MURDER IN MULESHOE

THE TEXAS PANHANDLE MURDERS

JACK R. STANLEY

WRIGHTBRIDGE PRESS

Published by Wrightbridge Press
4041 Appian Way
Arlington, TX 76013

Quantity sales. Special discounts are available on quantity purchases by corporations, associations, and others. For details, contact the publisher at the address above.

Printed in the United States of America

ISBN. 978-1-947726-49-9

DEDICATION

To the love of my life
Mary Lee
who makes all things possible.

2 Free Ebooks

ChroniclesMURDER IN MULESHOE
There's a killer in town. Do we hunt the S.O.B. down or throw him a
parade?

GUNS ALONG THE RIO
Two fresh-off-the-ranch 17-year-olds join the Texas Rangers in 1858.
What could possibly go wrong?

1

Jarvis Dickle was dead. Dead as a muleshoe nail --- which, ironically, is what killed him --- a nail used to hold a metal horseshoe in place --- only in this case, a muleshoe. Three muleshoe nails killed Jarvis to be exact. They were driven into his dirty, bald head.

His death was no big whoop and certainly no loss to anyone who knew him. Everybody in town registered somewhere on the dislike-to-down-right-loath scale for Jarvis Delmar Dickle. Even his daughter, pretty, divorced Lottie, a disc jockey and program director for the local A.M./F.M. radio station for Muleshoe, Texas, thought her old man was a world class asshole.

Now you have to understand that Muleshoe is a real place. It's more of a town than a city. The official population is just over five thousand, but that count must have been taken during the county fair. It was started in 1913 when the Pecos and Northern Texas Railroad put up an 88-mile line from Farwell to Lubbock. Okay, you've never heard of Farwell and most likely don't know Bailey County, but you should have heard of Lubbock. It's home to Texas Tech University for God's sake. All of this is up in what's called the Texas Panhandle --- but to folks who live there, it's just part of West Texas.

See, anything west of Ft. Worth --- "where the West begins" --- is considered West Texas --- including the Panhandle which to most yankees would be North Texas. But North Texas is Dallas and the area between there and Oklahoma.

Bailey County got its name from one of the defender of the Alamo, Peter James Bailey. If you don't know what the Alamo was and is, there's not much point in talking about it or Texas. Just skip ahead. The county is dry, meaning you can't buy alcoholic drinks there. No, not even Lone Star or Shiner beer --- which a lot of people in Texas consider extreme --- but that's Bailey County and Muleshoe. This is also dry land farming and ranching country, meaning the rain giveth and the dry West Texas winds taketh away.

Not that any of this had a damn thing to do with how Jarvis Dickle got nailed, but you can't grasp the people unless you know the county and the town.

Daughter Lottie Truett used her married name on-the-air. Even now, long after her cheating ex, Tagg Truett, had left. The story was Tagg was hit with a load of .12 gauge bird shot in the butt. He reportedly was trying to get into in his shiny ass into his Dodge dually with his pants still around his ankles at the moment he was tagged. He left town after he got out of the hospital. Lottie was in the studio and on-the-air like every day Monday thru Saturday 6 A.M. till 9, when Bailey County Sheriff, Asa Hunt, showed up.

Asa, all six feet six inches of lean leathered skin was tucked inside his khaki uniform. At 72, his polished custom made high top cowboy boots had two inch heels, he wore his nickel plated, hand engraved, Colt 1911 .45 semi-automatic on his hip, and he held his cream colored Resistol straw hat in his gnarled hands. Asa stood outside the double paned control room window until Lottie looked up and saw him. She motioned him in.

Down the hall Webb Fritz, owner and station owner and general manager, known to one and all, behind his back as "Wide-load," was getting himself his third cup of coffee of the day. This was part of his preparation to take the nine to noon shift on the air. He had a chubby handful of printed ag news in one hand as he waddled up to the control room window. He saw Lottie drop to her chair like she'd been poleaxed by a two by four at something the sheriff had just told her. As fast as he could, Webb hurried inside the studio.

"What's up?" the swaying, red faced owner asked in his God given round, deep and mellow baritone voice.

It took a second before Lottie looked over at her boss and said, "Webb. Maybe you can help me decide what song to play next."

"Huh???"

"I was thinkin' 'Dang Me, They Ought T' Take A Rope And Hang Me" --- or 'Drop Kick Me Jesus Through The Goalposts Of Life.'"

"What in the Sam Hill?" Webb asked.

Lottie began searching the CD stacked walls of the control room looking for music.

"Somebody killed Jarvis Dickle last night or early this morning," Sheriff Hunt said as Lottie moved out from between Webb and him. "But that's not for broadcast. I'm tryin' t' keep it quiet for a while."

"You lived in this town long, Asa?" the hefty station owner asked rhetorically. Asa Hunt had been in Muleshoe all his life and Sheriff for twenty-two years. It was a question but the sheriff still frowned rather than dignify it with an answer.

Webb absent mindedly watched Lottie as he spoke to the Sheriff again,

"Do you need Lottie for next-of-kin positive identification of the bastard?"

"It's procedure. I could have asked Mother Dickle --- but thought better of it."

"Lottie, you go." Webb said taking over the control room chair. "I got this covered," Webb set his news copy on the console in front of the audio board.

Lottie somehow got hold of herself and stepped back to Asa.

"And this is not for broadcast," the sheriff told Webb.

"It's news, Asa. That's our business. If I don't get it out before Inez Brinkley gets the word at the Coffee Mug, we might as well be the textbook business. Old news is just history. That's what Roman

Southmost prints once a week," referring to the weekly Muleshoe Express. "Express my ass."

"I don't want the damn perp to run."

"'Perp'? Do you think you're suddenly on C.S.I. Muleshoe?"

The sheriff just deepened his frown as he repeated, "I don't want him --- or her --- to run?"

"If you killed Jarvis Dickle, would you run --- or wait for the town to throw you a parade?" Webb turned to Lottie, "No offense, Lottie."

"None taken," she said. "I'd wait for a parade, too."

"And what jury in this county would vote to convict?" the radio station manager called as the sheriff led Lottie out the door.#

2

Jarvis' workshop was the last sliding door on a less than half full metal warehouse row of buildings about an eight of a mile outside the Muleshoe city limits. The asphalt drive way stopped just beyond his door, but the dirt and mud track continued on to a turnaround in a never plowed or harvested field. Attached to the side of Jarvis's signless business was a single gated, three rail, rust colored corral with shed. There were two dun colored jennies, female mules, standing in the shade of the shed near closed double doors which opened into the side of the shop.

It had started raining before sunrise for an hour and then drizzled for another thirty minutes eliminating any foot prints or muddy tire marks. Still there were two sheriff's patrol cars with their flashing lights attracting attention, and one from the town's Chief of Police, Luis Elizondo's office. All were keeping Jarvis's body from escaping the scene. The county's only coroner's truck and an ambulance also awaited events to move along.

A blanket was covering the body --- Lottie wondered if it were there to keep it warm on a day that would be in the 90's before sunset. Even the slab concrete floor, strewn with hey, was already hot. She could feel it through her boots. Both the front and back sliding doors

were open. Two six foot square Schaefer mobile box fans quietly
cranked away, one by each door. Both were aimed at center of the
shop where a furnace blazed, pulley hoists hung from the ceiling
crossbeams, and a dirty water trough sat near a classic blacksmith's
anvil.

"You know what those fans are for?" Lottie asked the casually
dressed Police Chief. His badge was embroidered on the left chest of
his blue shirt.

"To keep Jarvis cool I'd expect," the Chief answered.

"Nope. Jarvis didn't give a damn about his own comfort --- or
anybody else's. He bought'em and pointed to where his --- his equine
clients --- would be standing while he worked on them. He thought
more of mules than he did of people."

Luis Elizondo didn't know what to say to that. He looked over at
the sheriff.

Asa ushered Lottie over to the body and pulled back the blanket.

The three nails were still in his scalp and small drools of blood
seeped from each.

"That's my daddy," she said with no particular feeling.

Asa flipped the blanket back and nodded towards the County
Coroner, Dr. Betsy Sue Darvel, 40's, frumpy, always looked as if she
couldn't find or operate a comb or hairbrush. She and two ambulance
attendants stepped up to remove the body.

"Anything look out of place to you, Lottie," the sheriff asked?

"I've only been in here a half dozen times," the 27 year old said
looking around. A table held tools as did a pegboard four by eight
foot section of wall. "Usually I was pissed at Jarvis about something;
so I didn't pay much attention to the place." Still she gave the shop a
once over before saying, "Looks the same as always to me."

"Okay. Thanks for comin', hon."

"Glad t' do it," Lottie said kind of meaning it and kind of out of
her good natured habit.

Asa walked her over to the front door.

"Is this your case or Luis's?" she asked.

"Ours. We're just out of the city limits."

A Ford 250 pulling a double goose necked animal trailer pulled up outside the ring of official vehicles. Fifty-six year old, Hazen Snead, got out and strode over to Asa and Lottie. Hazen was a rancher from over in Clovis, N.M.

"Heard somebody murdered Jarvis," he said tipping his hat. "Sorry for your loss, Lottie."

"Thanks for the sentiment, Hazen, but we all knew Jarvis for what he was."

"Any ideas who done it?" he asked squinting at Asa.

"The usual suspects," the sheriff said. "Anybody who knew him."

"The whole damn town?"

"What are you doin' here, Hazen?"

"I came in to enjoy the ambiance of the big city. What do you think, Asa? Those are my jennies in the corral. They're mine. Brought them over first thing this morning."

"About what time?" Asa asked turning his head to favor his good left ear.

"Oh, I got them out of the trailer damn near 6:30 --- 6:45. It was still raining."

"And you just left them?"

"Jarvis and I have a deal," Hazen said looping his thumbs in his suspenders over his faded blue and red patterned shirt. "He works on my animals and I pay whatever he asks --- in cash --- when I pick'em up."

"So he didn't have to declare any more than he wanted. Cheated the government, I'll bet?"

"Yeah. It's not like the government's ever bent us over a barrel an' took what they wanted? If he found a way t' screw the I.R.S., that makes him a better man than I thought."

"Were the doors open when you got here?"

"Nope. I figured he hadn't opened up yet. I like it that way and so does he. The less we see of each other, the better. I went for breakfast over at the Coffee Cup. That's where I heard the news on the radio."

"I knew Wideload couldn't keep his mouth shut."

"Inez was cussin' him, too. You know she like to know everything first."

Asa just shook his head.

"Mind if I get my mules? Or are they suspects too? Need to finger print'em?" Hazen asked.

"What is it about being around Jarvis, dead or alive, that makes everyone a smart ass?"

"Coodies or horseflies?"

"Go to hell, Hazen."

"It's called New Mexico. And I'll go if I can I take my mules?"

"Go ahead on. Your asses are the only ones around who likely didn't kill Jarvis."#

3

"I need to go talk with Mother Dickle," Lottie told Asa as Hazen got in his truck and backed his trailer up to the gate.

"So do I," the Sheriff said. "But I've got to stick around here a while."

"I'm sure she'll be expecting you."

"Yeah, I think so, too. Guess chances are she knows already. If she didn't hear Webb on the radio, somebody will have called her by now. What is it with old divorcees, widows, spinsters and gossip?"

"I guess you'll find out soon enough."

"Lottie, you're never going to be one of them. Some nice, smart young fella's goin' snatch you up and you'll have a good life, yet."

"I think I've been snatched up enough for one lifetime. As long as my taste in men runs towards the likes of Tagg Truett, I'm better off alone."

Asa didn't know what to say to that.

"Well, tell Maude --- ." he began and then stopped. "Oh, hell, I don't know what t' tell her." Asa was one of the few who were contemporaries of Jarvis's mother to call her by her first name. Most folks called her Mother Dickle.

"She'll know," Lottie said. "I'm wonderin' what I'm goin' t' say to her."

"She's your grandmother. She loves you."

"Question is, did she love my daddy? I don't think so --- and I don't blame her." Lottie turned to her truck, but over her shoulder she said, "You know where you can find me."

"I'm sure there will be more questions."

"I don't know I'll have any more answers."

Lottie climbed in her rusty and sun bleached red GMC pick-up and fished through her purse looking for her keys. She located them and jammed the right one into the ignition. But she didn't crank the engine and add to its ninety-six thousand miles, just yet. She just sat there watching Asa walk back to her father's place of business and the scene of his death.

She was twenty-eight but with just a touch of make-up could still pass for nineteen. High apple cheeks under a smooth, pale complexion, buff flaxen hair cut short against the Texas heat, and deep set green eyes were only part of what make Lottie Truett a looker --- in spite of her usual uniform of jeans, boots and plain front, logoless, print free, decoration lacking, extra-extra-large T-shirt. The feature which had seemed to define Lottie were her large breasts --- and firm, narrow hips. The total package was all woman. She always wore a sleeveless denim vest which disgusted her forty-two D's and held her licensed concealed carry .9 mm pistol on an inside pocket.

Her wild youth, one dismal marriage, and a soul sucking divorce had taken their toll more inside than out. She felt rode hard and put up wet as she slumped against the steering wheel until it burned her forearms and she jerked back up. She cranked the ol' truck until the engine finally caught and began to settle into its normal shivering rattle. If life had taught her anything, it was that bad things didn't get any better by trying to put them off.

The Police Chief got into his car, turned off his flashing lights, and drove back to town before she could move.

Lottie stomped in the clutch to the floor and forced the transmission into low with the floor mounted shifter and headed out of town west on U.S. Highway 70. She took the dirt road north and drove the mile and a quarter to what everyone knew as the Dickle Place.

The two story old ranch house hadn't seen a coat of paint in Lottie's lifetime. It wasn't so much run-down as it was used well past its expiration date. Untrimmed grass encircled the low front porch where a rusty glider porch swing sat.

On the glider with a glass of iced tea in a weathered and wrinkled hand was Maude Dickle. She wore a cotton house dress over her ample busted body, along with scuffed cowboy boots while she played with her curly salt and pepper hair and looked off in the distance at nothing. She was both willowy and tough at the same time the way many West Texas women tend to be. Her grey eyes looked through plastic tortoise shell frames on either side of a small, ski jump nose. She had been pretty in her younger years. What one saw now wasn't the wrinkles or the age spots, but the softness, the kindness, just beneath a hard exterior.

She didn't look over at Lottie as her granddaughter's pickup rattled up and stopped. Her eyes never changed their focus as the younger woman climbed the wooden steps and sat down on the weather beaten porch rail near the glider.

"You saw him?" she asked after a moment.

"Asa came to the station and got me --- took me over there. Whoever did it, killed him in his shop. Both doors were open. I'd say they snuck up behind him while he was firing up the furnace. Somehow they managed to drive three muleshoe nails right in the top of his head."

Maude continued to rock on the glider a few minutes.

"Who told you, Nana?"

"Caroline called." Caroline Montoya was Maude's best friend.

Maude looked up at Lottie.

"How are you doin'?"

"I'm all right. You know we didn't have much to do with each other. He's like a stranger to me. A stranger I didn't much like."

"That's the way he wanted it, I think."

"Why?"

"He wasn't like that before he went to war. 'Course, you were too little to remember. Your mama was already sick then. She was dead before he got out and came home."

"Couldn't he have gotten out of goin'? Compassionate leave, or something?"

"Would you?"

"Well, sure."

"Think about it, hon. You ever dodged a bad thing in your life? No. You step up and take it. You got that from him. Not that he didn't want t' say, "No" --- but it wasn't his way. Your momma knew it, too. They didn't even talk about it. His number was up --- it was his turn t' go --- so he went."

Mother Dickle looked off in the distance again.

"It was the war and your mother's death that did it --- flipped a switch somewhere inside him. I used to say he had P.T.S.O.B. That was him, Post Traumatic Son-of-a-Bitch."

"Nana, you know what that makes you?"#

4

"Hon, I've been a bitch all my life," Mother Dickle said. "I was a bitchy little kid --- when I discovered sex they thought I was a bitch-in-heat. 'Fore your grandpaw and I got married they me a 'bitchy bride.' Even today, every time I go into protest my taxes they all says, 'Oh, hell, here comes that ol' bitch, again'."

"But you've never been like that to me?" Lottie said still sitting on the porch rail.

"Cause I always thought you had it hard enough. What with losing your mother so early --- and Jarvis being the way he was --- I tried very hard not to be just one more burr under your blanket."

"Well, everybody in this town loves you."

"They put up with me. It ain't the same thing."

"No, they love you. How many stray kids have you taken in over the years?"

"It's a big ol' house. I thought it shouldn't go t' waste."

"Six that I know of. And only one of them every ended up in trouble."

"Pollard shouldn't have gotten arrested. He was 15, got drunk 'cause his daddy didn't get paroled. They arrested him for takin' a leak on a stop sign. How many other 15 year-olds have gotten drunk and peed on something but nothin' ever happened to them? Even I did."

"Nana? I don't believe it."

"It's the God's truth. I got drunk, parked just beyond the city limits and walked back and peed on the city limits sign when I 16. I was so tired of this one mule town. It was Asa Hunt who tried to arrest me. He was working as a patrolman for th' town back then. But I walked back to my car and I was out of his jurisdiction and we both knew it. He wanted to come after me. Guess he realized claimin' t' be in 'hot pursuit' wouldn't wash with the judge. Besides, I think he just wanted to know if I was wearin' panties or not --- I wasn't."

"I drove over t' Springlake, up to Dimmitt, across t' Bovina and down t' Farwell and came back into town from the other side."

"He didn't wait for you on the road to the house from the highway?"

"Oh, sure. But I drove through Burley Keiber's back forty and Asa never saw me. He was mad at me for years over that."

She took a sip of her iced tea.

"Anyway, I always thought that pissin' arrest was what started Pollard down the road to joinin' his ol' man in prison."

A shiny Chevy sedan came up the road toward the house.

"That'll be the first of the church ladies' casserole caravan."

Lottie shaded her eyes and looked at the car.

"Look's like Gloria Clift." Florid skinned, eighty-one year old Gloria Clift was the widow of late Baptist preacher, Brother Edwin Clift

"By the middle of the afternoon there will be enough food in here to feed a posse."

"They's tryin t' be nice, Nana."

"And nosey. They want to be the first one to know any gossip."

"Their hearts' are in the right place?"

"You can't say the same thing for the rest of their anatomy. Mona Purifoy has been nipped and tucked, botoxed and siliconed to where I'll bet St. Peter'll have no idea who the hell she is."

"Mona will never die, Nana. She will just keep replacing and recycling parts."

"I hear Frank has an inventory of Mona parts that's as big as his whole Mahindra dealership."

The pair shared a laugh.

Heavy set Gloria Clift parked in the grass and pulled her figure out of the Chevy, fished a bunt cake from the backseat and started up the path to the house. Lottie met her halfway and took the cake. They continued on together.

"Looks like I'm the first one here besides you, dear," the wrinkled and overly rouged faced lady said.

"Yes'am," Lottie said with the cake in on hand and the elderly woman's elbow in her other.

"That's why I baked a bunt. They're quick --- and about all I can manage these days."

"We appreciate it."

"Maude," Mrs. Clift called as they approached.

"Gloria," came the answer without Maude Dickle moving from the glider.

"Sorry to hear about Jarvis's passing."

"He didn't pass, Gloria. Somebody nailed his ass --- and not in a good way."

"Is there such a thing as a 'good way'?" Lottie helped the minister's wife up the wooden steps.

"Used to be," Maude said, "--- but I was a lot younger then."

"Shame on you, Maude, for even thinkin' such things."

Mona was still arranging herself and her dress before turning toward the house.

Lottie helped the visitor into a rusted porch rocker.

"Never been married to a preacher. I don't have t' watch what I think or say. And when you give it a thought, didn't Jesus get nailed in a good way --- for our sakes?"

"You think of the strangest things, Maude. And then you say them. I don't know if you're being honest, blaspheming, or simply trying to make trouble."

"A little of all three," Maude said.

"Well, no matter how you say it, I'm sorry Jarvis was killed. It's my Christian duty to say so."

"When was the last time you had a good thing to say about Jarvis?" Maude asked. "Or anybody in this town, for that matter."

"God bless him. Jarvis didn't make it easy."

"Isn't your Christian duty to love him anyway?"

"We did, Maude."

"The hell you did. And nobody liked him. *I* didn't like him much myself."

"But you did love him. Because it was your duty as a mother."

"Are you two going to argue about this all day?" Lottie finally asked.

"Better than lyin' to each other," Maude said.

"I didn't come here to argue. I brought you a cake."

"Well, thank you, Gloria. The first thing I thought when Caroline called and said Jarvis was killed was, 'Damn it! I need a cake.'"

Three more vehicles, including a sparkling Cadillac SUV, an extended cab Dodge, and Honda minivan made the trek up towards the house.

"That'll be Mona Purifoy in her Escalade," Lottie said. Granddaughter and grandmother exchanged knowing smiles.

"So, it begins," Maude said.#

5

"I have to ask," Asa said when he and Maude were alone and the horde of church ladies were busy making the inside of the house look acceptable by their standards. "Where were you this morning --- between five and seven?"

"You mean did I kill Jarvis?"

"That's not what I asked," the lanky sheriff was holding his hat in his hands.

"But it's what you mean. I was here, Asa, and since Lottie moved out, there's been nobody else to testify about my morning habits or whereabouts. I didn't like my son --- but he was my son --- and I didn't kill him."

"Sorry to have to put you through this."

"Not your fault, Asa --- unless you killed him."

"Like damn near everybody else, I avoided contact with Jarvis whenever possible. Did you know if he paid any federal taxes?"

"You workin' for the feds now, Asa?"

"I'm only askin' 'cause Hazen Snead pointed out that Jarvis only dealt in cash."

"So? Are there any I.R.S. agents in town?"

"Not that I know of."

"That your best motive so far?"

"So far. Being an ass shouldn't be enough to get anybody killed. Not around here."

"Speak for yourself."

"I am. There are a lot of people who are hacked at me for arresting them for bein' drunk …"

"And pissin' on city limits signs?"

Asa couldn't keep a straight face for more than a couple of seconds.

"I never arrested you, Maude."

"Not that you didn't want to?"

"If we're bein' perfectly honest here," Asa grinned, "that's not what I wanted."

"Oh, I know what you wanted, Asa. And if you hadn't been such a goodie goodie, you might have got some."

"I was trying to be a good cop. And back in those days I thought it meant making everybody obey each and every law on the books."

"When did you wise up?"

"In the service. I was an M.P. and had a major set me straight one night when we were about to bust a whore house in Korea."

"You didn't bust down the doors and haul the girls off and pitch all the men in the stockade?"

"I wanted to. 'Thought that's what being a cop, military or civilian, was all about. The major said, 'Keepin' the peace is more than busting heads and clamping on handculfs.' Said, 'Sometimes being a good cop means lookin' the other way --- driving around the block instead of pulling somebody over --- letting people make their own mistakes without adding jail time to their miseries. Being a *peace officer* isn't always about right and wrong. He reminded me of the story of Solomon and the baby with two mothers. Peace and justice,' he told me, 'are what our job is. Keep the peace and try to let justice be done.' That's what I tried to do with Jarvis. I knew he was often spoiling for a fight --- so I didn't give him one if I could help it."

"And now somebody's killed him."

"And somebody is going to pay for it. Jarvis had a miserable life and I tried not to contribute to it --- but he didn't deserve to be murdered."

"If we weren't s' damn old, Asa, I might let you get what you wanted s' long ago."

"But we are damned old, Maude --- and I'm still married."

"I wouldn't do Kathy Lou wrong for anything."

"Neither would I."

DOWN AT THE Coffee Mug Inez Brinkley was topping off "Wideload" Webb Fritz's cup. The corpulent owner/manager of the radio station was sitting at a table --- he'd given up on booths which he really preferred because he could no longer fit between the table and the seat.

"Who's on the air?" the small breasted waitress asked as she gave Wideload a good long flash of less than ample cleavage.

"The second Ohlendorf boy. Simon."

"The pizza faced one?"

"He's got a good voice and he learns quick."

"And he's got a face for radio," Turner Ratleff the big mustached, gap toothed and hawk nosed owner of Ratleff Hardware said from the counter where he was eating a chicken pot pie. Ever since his divorce three years ago, he had come to depend on Inez and the Coffee Mug for most of his meals.

Virge Barlow, the skinny Coffee Mug cook who always looked as if he didn't eat much of his own cooking, leaned through the horizontal pass through. "Any news about Jarvis?"

"Asa's not talking," Wideload said, "and neither is Betsy Sue." He was referring to the Chief and the county medical examiner, Dr. Betsy Sue Darvel.

"But she is doin' an autopsy ain't she?" Inez asked.

"Has, too," Wideload said enjoying the attention of being the focal point of all the conversation. "Any suspicious death requires an autopsy by law."

"What's suspicious about it? He got three nails in the head, didn't he?" Virge asked.

"But Asa has no suspects. That's suspicious enough."

"We should start a pool," the cook went on grabbing a clean coffee mug from his side of the pass through. "Bet on who did it --- or take up a reward for whoever did it."

"Virge," Inez scolded. "That's a nasty thing t' say."

"Nasty? Why? You like Jarvis, Inez? Was there somethin' going on we didn't know about?"

"Don't make me sick," she shot back. "Jarvis Dickle? God!"

"So what's it going to be --- a pool or a reward?"#

6

"I had turned my radio off and was listin' to music on my phone." Dallas said. "Didn't know about it until Judd told me after I landed." Judd was the mechanic for Dallas's yellow and blue AT-602 Air Tractor crop duster. He was also the drummer in Dallas's band.

"There wasn't anything you could have done," Lottie said as he held her in his arms.

Dallas Kerkendall was six years younger than Lottie, but with his baby face he looked like a teenager in spite of towering over her at six foot two. He was deeply tanned with dark blue eyes and modest sandy colored hair peeking out from under his N.R.A. baseball cap. He wore cowboy boots, jeans, and a slightly plaid shirt over his solid arms.

"I could have been with you," he said.

"I had to deal with Asa and Nana. He needed me to identify Daddy's body in his shop and Nana had church casserole ladies swarm her all day."

"How are you doing?"

"Numb. I think I should be feeling something --- but I'm really not."

"I had a friend who lost his mother and went through the funeral, the will, settling her estate and amazed everyone at how he held up. Then one day --- about a year later, he was out fishing on Coyote Lake by himself and it hit him --- his mother was dead. He told me he cried like a baby --- for hours. He almost couldn't load up his boat when he came back in."

"Well, that's something to look forward to."

"What I'm trying to tell you is that everybody deals with these things differently. Whenever it sneaks up and hits you, babe, I want you to know I'm here for you."

"I know," she said kissing him.

"Is there anything I can do for you?" he asked when they parted.

"How about we shower together and then go to bed?"

He picked her up in his arms and headed for the bathroom in her small two bedroom frame duplex.

"You don't have to ask me twice," he smiled.

As Dallas was soaping her up, Lottie said, "You know, people think I'm robbing the cradle."

"Screw'em," he said. "We're both old enough to drink and vote."

"And screw," she joked. "You don't think I'm too old for you?"

"Lottie, the only thing you're robbing is my sperm bank. And I'm your willing ATM. Now, will you marry me?"

"No, I will not marry you, Dallas. Do we have to do this now?" Standing covered only in suds, Lottie looked up a her significant other, Dallas Kerkendall, also naked standing in the shower with her. "I thought you wanted to make me feel better?"

"I can't do that as your husband? Come on, make an honest man out of me. My mother thinks we're living in sin."

"We're living in half a duplex on West Avenue J. Your mother lives in Seattle. Sin is two blocks over."

"If you're talkin' about Sabi Trejo's girls --- they work for their money."

"You better not know that from firsthand experience?"

"Sorry, Lottie. But once upon a time I was an All-State football star. Where do you think they took me to celebrate?"

She frowned as he laughed.

"If it makes you feel any better, I was so drunk by then the only thing I could get up was my supper and beer."

Lottie had to smile at that.

"Was this before or after the game they threw you out of?"

In a state championship series, Dallas had been ejected for "Unsportsmen Like Conduct." He had clipped a linebacker from the other team and broke the guy's leg.

"Hey, I still think he deserved it. He blindsided Daryle Tolie in the play before --- and Daryle had already thrown the ball. None of the refs seemed to notice that."

"But his leg break kept him out of the NFL for a year."

"Look, the NFL never wanted *me*. And after he made it, he only played three games and was benched for costing the Colts a game for doing the same thing he did to Daryle. He was a dirty player."

"And you weren't?"

"When the occasion demanded. Don't get me mad. And, by the way, it's not like you were untouched by human hands when we met?"

"Okay, okay."

"You are jealous. I like that," Dallas laughed. "A marriage license would fix that?"

"What makes you think so? What is a marriage license? A license to sleep together? We don't need it. A license to fight? We're doing that right now. A license to have children? I can't have children. We don't need it."

"A license to get old together. A license for us to know that neither of us is going anywhere. We're here for each other. Now and until death do us part?"

"Been there --- done that. It doesn't work. And frankly, I'm glad it didn't. Look at Tagg Truett. If I'd stayed with him one --- or both of us would be dead by now. Look at my Daddy. Dallas, I have terrible taste in men."

"That include me?"

"Ask your mother. Do you think she's ever coming back from Seattle?"

"Never."

"So if your mother doesn't want to be near you --- you're either another mistake I've made --- or there's something about you I don't know, yet."

"Lottie, what's wrong with me is that I'm in love with an older woman who isn't sure about me. She thinks it's all a MILF thing but it's the real thing. I love you."

"I love you, too, Dallas. I think you're too good to be true. Let's not spoil it with marriage. I'm neurotic and paranoid for both of us. "

"Okay --- for now," he said grabbing her by the butt and lifting her up so she wrapped her legs around his waist. "But I'm not giving up --- and, as you can tell," he said wiggling into position. In a moment they were flying united. "I'm not letting you off the hook on this."

"Since you put it that way," she said looping her arms around his neck and smiling wickedly, "We can talk about this again --- later --- much, much later." She kissed him.

WHEN THE ALARM WENT OFF, both Lottie and Dallas knew it was 4 AM. Five days a week they both woke to another work day --- for Lottie, working in local radio, it was six day --- including Saturday. This was Thursday. She showered alone and when she turned the water off, it was Dallas's signal to go put the coffee on. By the time she emerged from the bathroom, he was holding a steaming cup for her as they kissed and passed, he into the bath, and she to get dressed.

At the radio station Lottie discovered a still sleeping seventeen year old Simon Ohlendorf on the lobby couch. The young nerd with a very mature voice and a bad case of acne was so tall his feet hung off the end of the couch, and he snuggled into the cushions. Lottie liked the kid. He was quick to pick up on everything and ran the station pretty much all by himself on Sundays --- mostly riding the network all day after carrying the Baptist church service. He read a few news summaries from the Associated Press, the local weather and did the obligatory half hour station breaks as required by the FCC.

Lottie didn't turn on any lights in the lobby or the hallway, instead just fliped on the control room overheads and those in the break room where she started a first pot of coffee of the day. She flipped on the big toggle switch at the bottom of the remote equipment rack and turned on the transmitter located a quarter mile away behind the studio in a windowless cinderblock building with the antenna shoved into the air two-hundred feet beside it.

Next she turned on the two flat screens and the computer beside the audio console with sliding knobs like you see in recording studios. There was a single mic suspended over the console, or the "board" as everyone called it. A short equipment rack held three CD players and three other stacks of necessary gear, including a separate rack behind the main one. The walls were loaded with CD's of every country music artist since the 50's. A large double paned window looked out on the hallway, the inside pane was a mass of Scotch taped memo's and official FCC notices, some of them turning yellow with age.

When the second hand on the pulsating wall clock above the flat screens ticked to five AM, Lottie opened the mic and said, "Good morning, Muleshoe! We're starting another wonderful day in the Texas Panhandle." She clicked the mouse and the curser blinked on one of the flat screens and the Star Spangle Banner began to broadcast.

Everyone who was tuned in wondered, "What's Lottie doing at work this morning?"#

7

It was only a few seconds into the National Anthem when Simon Ohlendorf yanked open the door wiping his eyes with the back of his hand.

"Ms. Lottie, what are you doing here? I'm supposed to cover for you?"

"Simon, you're still growing and you need your sleep. Go home. I'm fine."

"But your daddy....," he didn't know how to politely say what he needed to.

"He's just as dead now as he was yesterday. It's all in the Sheriff's hands. Nothing I can do."

"But what about Mother Dickle?"

"I sure Caroline Montoya spent the night with her. Together they'll do whatever needs to done." Caroline Montoya was Maude's best friend and had been since they started kindergarten together. Over the years, Caroline was a more regular church goer than Maude, the local wild child. But what Maude had done for the abandoned children of the town after she lost her husband, Jasper, was more than Caroline could have ever done.

Still they were a good fit. Tiny Caroline McKinny had been a wallflower and total introvert until day three of kinder when Maude latched onto her. It happened the first time one of the Kelso boys had tried picking on the shy little girl. Maude jumped into the middle of his business, and he was the one who crawled away crying while Maude was hauled to the principal's office.

In high school Caroline was shocked by what Maude would do, but their friendship could not be broken. It had been Caroline to had called Maude with the news about Jarvis' murder. She had arthritis and it was hard for her to move; so she didn't make it to Maude's house until after most of the church ladies had descended. Caroline had lost her husband, Santo Mantoya, when he was thrown from a spooked horse. He lingered almost a year before dying in his bed with Caroline at his side.

"But Mr. Fritz asked me to fill in for you," Simon pleaded.

"Not necessary. I'll tell Webb I sent you home. I'm sure he still wants you to work tonight."

Simon had become somewhat of a celebrity by virtue of being on the air. He was still a lanky nerd but now there was something more to him that the girls his age were seeing. Lottie was glad to see the young man come out of his shell. He even stood taller and straighter these days. It was his senior year in high school, and she expected his acne to clear up once he started getting laid.

SHERIFF ASA HUNT phoned the station to tell Lottie that Dr. Betsy Sue Darvel, the frumpy county coroner, had finished the autopsy on Jarvis' body.

"She find out anything?"

"Nope," Asa said. "It was those three nails that killed him just like we thought."

"Any new suspects or do you figure the family is still your best bet?"

"Lottie, don't be like that. I'm just trying to follow procedures. This is only the third murder mystery I've ever had. Every other killing has either been a bar fight, a husband catching his wife in bed with somebody else --- or vice versa --- something where it was always clear who shot who. But not this time."

"Wish I could help you, Asa, but you know how Daddy was --- with Nana and me."

"And everyone else."

"Well, you didn't call to tell me nothing. What do I need to know?"

"Do I call Zollman's --- or what do you want to do?"

The Zollman family had owned the local funeral home since before God made West Texas dust.

"I guess. We've still got plots out at Oakwood Lawns. Daddy could go right beside Momma."

"There's no need for you or Maude to come claim the body unless you want to. I can just turn it over to Zollman's."

"I'll give Beatrice a call."

"When I get more news, I'll be sure to let you know, Lottie."

"Thanks, Asa. I know you have a job to do and I'm not trying to make it harder."

"Appreciate that, Lottie."

She hung up and found Zollman's phone number on-line and called.

Beatrice was a year younger than Lottie. When she went goth in high school, nobody was surprised. Death was the family business. She had grown out of it after college and had taken over the funeral business a couple of years back. She looked oriental because her mother was a Vietnam war bride of her father, a supply sergeant stationed in Cam Rahn Bay. Beatrice was a beauty, but because of the Zollman name and business she didn't have a lot of friends growing up. She and Lottie hung out every once and a while through high school but were never really close. Lottie was wild and Beatrice wasn't willing to express her teen angst in the same way.

Their phone conversation was short and professional. Beatrice accepted the job and dispatched a hearse to the morgue to pick up Jarvis' body. She promised to get back in touch with both Lottie and

Maude when they felt ready to deal with arrangements. Lottie mentioned the plot the family owned and Beatrice said she'd take it from there.

Lottie read the local weather forecast on the hour and read a few news headlines over the air before returning to playing country music.

"Wideload" Webb Fritz ambled in and went straight to the coffee pot where Lottie joined him.

"I told Simon to go home. I was up anyway --- and there's nothing else for me to do."

"Maude doesn't need you?"

"Don't think so. Caroline's with her."

"Plus the church ladies."

"There is that, too."

Just then a rumble of motorcycles shook the building. Lottie and Webb walked to the front door to see the thundering mass of about fifty high end, customized Harleys rumble down the street, a large Confederate battle flag, a Texas flag, and 'Ol Glory fluttered from different bikes.

"What the hell?" Webb asked.#

8

L ottie hurried over to the corner of South Main and East Avenue C --- the location of the Muleshoe Police Department. There was simply no way for "Wideload" to hurry anywhere beyond a few feet. Even getting into his truck would have taken more time than it took Lottie to drive from the studio over to where the fifty-something Harley-Davidsons were parked.

One police officer was standing on the landing looking down on the parking lot filled with now silent bikes. Three of the riders had taken the stairs and were waiting there with the patrolman when Chief Luis Elizondo stepped outside and joined the group. This happened as Lottie was climbing out of her pick up and headed toward the action.

On the back of the leather vests all the riders wore was a Confederate Battle Flag with a rifle telescope view on top with the crosshairs centered over the star in the middle of the flag. Around each telescope were the stitched letters which read, "Texas Rebel Snipers." These were the TRS. Each rider had a scope mounted rifle slung over their backs with the barrels pointed down. Each also wore a semi-automatic or revolver pistol in holsters on their belts. The three riders talking to the Chief and his officer had left their rifles in rifle scabbards across their handle bars of their bikes. Texas has been an open carry state for a while; so intimidating as these armed men might have been, they were not violating the law in the least.

As Lottie climbed the side steps to the landing and flipped on the video recorder of her cell phone, Police Chief Elizondo was speaking into his cell.

"Asa," he said. "Can you come over to my shop? There are some people here who want to go see Jarvis' mother." He paused and then said, "We'll be here." He clicked off his phone.

"Sheriff Hunt should be here in a couple of minutes."

"We'll wait," the leader, a deeply tanned man with salt and pepper hair, said. The man, like most of the others on the cycles, wore a beard and or mustache.

"Chief Elizondo," Lottie said into her phone, recording their conversation for possible later broadcast. Whatever this was, it was news. "What's going on here?"

"Lottie," the 45 year old, muscular chief said noticing her approaching. "This is Spencer Lydecker," he introduced the leader who wore camo, his last name stitched above his left top pocket and a major's gold oak leaf on his right collar. "He is looking for Jarvis' home."

"I can show them his trailer," Lottie said.

"--- and his family," the Chief added.

Lottie looked at the man but she didn't say anything.

"Sheriff Hunt is on his way over here."

Lottie swung her phone's camera to the parking lot and the platoon of bikers stood tall beside their hogs.

A matter of moments later Asa's SUV squealed to a halt at the curb, and he swung down with his hat on. He took his time striding up to the chief, Lottie, and the three biker gang leaders.

"Sheriff," the big man standing in front of the police chief offered his hand to Asa.

Without hesitation, the sheriff took the proffered hand saying, "Major Lydecker, is it?"

Shaking the sheriff's hand the man said, "Spencer Lydecker.

Retired, sir. The Chief of Police says this is a county jurisdiction matter."

"That's right. What is your interest in it?"

"We're up from Houston, Sheriff. Our organization is here to see that Lt. Dickle is given the full honors he is due?"

"Honors?"

"Lt. Dickle was one of us. A sniper."

"You are aware that Jarvis Dickle was murdered?"

"Yes, sir. And we do *not* want to interfere with your investigation, Sheriff. If possible, we'd even like to offer our help if there is anything we can do."

"That won't be necessary." Asa told Lydecker.

"Is if possible for us to meet Lt. Dickle's family? We understand his mother has a ranch near here."

Asa and Lottie exchanged looks before the Sheriff took matters into his hands.

"She does. You can follow me and I'll lead you out to her ranch."

"Anything I can do?" Chief Elizondo asked.

"Give Maude a call and let her know we're coming."

"Will do."

"Lottie, do you want to ride out with me?" Asa asked her.

"Yes," she said.

"Do me a favor," the sheriff said. "As we move through the city, let's not make it 'rolling thunder.'"

"We can do that," Lydecker said as he turned to those below. "Keep it down!" he said.

Lottie got into Asa's SUV and the cyclists followed them out to Maude's house. The Chief of Police served as a rear guard.

Maude Dickle, her .12 gauge under her arm, and her friend Caroline Montoya in her walker, were standing on Maude's front porch as the whole parade came up the dirt road and stopped in the weeds beyond the church ladies sedans and SUVs. There was fright in the eyes of the other women who chose to stay inside while Maude looked as if she was ready to take on the whole lot.

Asa and Lottie led Lydecker and two other similarly dressed men up to the bottom of the steps.

Maude had her arms crossed, shotgun hanging across her forearm in the crook of her elbow, its barrels aimed down toward the warped porch steps. Her eyes narrowed as the sheriff spoke.

"Mrs. Dickle, this is retired Major Spencer Lydecker."

"Speak your piece," Maude said.

"Pardon the intrusion, Mrs. Dickle. I know what we look like --- but there's more here than meets the eye."

"I sure as hell hope so. I'm not overwhelmed by a bunch of men who haven't seen a barber or the working side of a razor in a coon's age, and have nothing better to do with their time than ride around on motorcycles tryin' t' scare the crap out of old bitches like me."

"Please forgive our appearance. Not a man here ever met or knew your son --- but we are his brothers in arms. And through that, maybe we knew him better than anyone else alive."

"Are you sure? My son was an asshole --- to me --- to his wife --- to his daughter," she motioned toward Lottie, "and to everybody who knew him."

"You're Lt. Dickle's daughter?" Lydecker asked Lottie.

"I never knew him as a Lt. I hardly knew him as a father."

"Then we *do* know him better than either of you."#

9

The church ladies suddenly all had a prayer meeting somewhere off Maude's ranch. Sheriff Hunt and Chief Elizondo stayed for about a half hour before returning to town. Before they left, with Maude's permission, some of the TRS boys dug a hole in her front yard and erected an aluminum flag pole. They produced a couple of bags of ready mix and poured concrete around the pole securing it.

"When it's dry--- by the morning, we'll run up a flag. The local V.F.W. will see to it every day," Spencer Lydecker said.

"You asked'em?" Maude asked.

"Not yet. But we will. And they'll be happy to do it?"

"I don't think you know everybody in our VFW," Asa said.

"It doesn't matter, Sheriff. They'll do it."

"If you're planning on starting something down at the VFW ...."

"We're not here to cause trouble," Lydecker looked up at Maude and Lottie, "--- not for anyone."

About half the riders mounted up and rode out. Those who remained dismounted.

"Ma'am," Lydecker said to Maude, "you mind if we tidy up a little out here?"

"Whatever makes you happy."

"Tools in the barn?"

"Yup. And rusted up tight. That mower ain't been started in years."

"It will do," Lydecker said his dark eyes reassuring.

Their leader only had to nod to his men before they headed for the barn.

"You think you'll be all right, Maude?" the sheriff asked.

"Oh, I think these boys and I will get along fine," she said laying her shotgun across the rusted arms of one of the front porch chairs.

LOTTIE RODE BACK to the radio station with Asa. They noted that several of the TRS bikes were parked in spaces in front of Chuy Varga's barber shop. When she got out of the sheriff's SUV, he said, "I'll come by this evening just to check on things."

"Thank you, Sheriff," Lottie said climbing down and closing the door.

She put together a new story with a sound bite from the front of the Police Department. It was the lead story on the 6 PM news.

"That wasn't thunder you heard rumbling through Muleshoe late this morning. It was the Texas Rebel Snipers --- a motorcycle club of former military snipers from Houston. According to their leader, retired major Spencer Lydecker, the group is here in the Panhandle to pay full military honors to Jarvis Dickle who was found murdered in his workshop on Tuesday morning. The group paid a visit to the Dickle ranch and spoke to Mother Maude Dickle."

Lottie played the clip of dialogue where Lydecker was speaking to Maude on her front porch.

"While it is well known that the murdered mule farrier had served in Afghanistan before returning to Muleshoe several years ago, few knew he was a lieutenant or much about his service. It was a subject Dickle didn't like to talk about even to his family.

"The former military men have erected a flagpole in front of the

Dickle home and plan to be at the funeral tomorrow afternoon at
2 PM."

THE SPUTTERING and then steady running of the old lawn mower
caused Maude and her friend Caroline to exchange looks of surprise.

"Well, I'll be damned," Maude said.

"We both will be most likely," Caroline grinned.

"If I get there first, I'll save you a seat by the fire."

A couple of the men were swinging rusty cycles with newly
polished and sharped edges while three others had found some paint
and were working on the house. A group returned from town all
sheared and clipped. They took over the jobs already started by some
who had remained and a second group rode out.

"You boys do this often?" Maude asked Lydecker who was oiling
the hinge of the gate.

"Not so such."

"Why this time?"

Lydecker stood up and said, "You really don't know, do you?"

"Know what?"

"Who your son was?"

"I know he was one ornery, piss ant who didn't have a decent
word for anybody in the town. I've often wondered why he came
back. He couldn't even take time off from that damn war to come
home when his wife died."

"One thing you figure out in big hurry over there, ma'am, is that
there's not a Goddamn thing you can do for the dead. It's the living
you can help. It's the living you can make a difference for. 'Cause once
you're dead --- you're beyond our reach."

"It sounds to me like there's a whole lot you know about my son
that I don't. When are you plannin' t' tell me."

"This evening --- when your granddaughter comes back. I think
she should know who he was, too."

Maude sat back but said nothing else.

It was past nine in the evening when Lottie, Maude, Caroline, Lydecker and another man, introduced as Sergeant-Major Luke Narvaez, a dark skinned Hispanic with a scar on one cheek, and one white eye brow. Both men had been shaved but kept their mustaches, both within military specs.

"You boys clean up nice," Maude said as she picked up the now empty plates, and Lottie cut big slices of chocolate cake. "And you have good appetites. Both are good signs as far as I'm concerned."

"The men will likely put a big dent in that spread you put out," Lydecker said nodding toward the dining room where others of their group came and went getting refills from the buffet laid out there.

This smaller group ate at the kitchen table.

"You'll like that cake," Caroline said. "Mona Purifoy may look like a walking plastic surgeon's mistake, but she makes one heck of a Milky Way cake. She likes to call it a 'Better Than Sex' cake and nobody wants to tell her she's got her recipes mixed up."

When Maude and Lottie had taken their seats again, Maud said, "Let's have it. What do I not know about my son-of-a-bitch son --- and, yes, I know --- I'm the bitch."#

10

Spencer Lydecker picked up a folder he had put under his chair when he sat down to eat. He opened it for reference on the Formica top table.

"When Jarvis Dickle reported for his last tour of duty, he was an Infantry Staff Sergeant. His MOS, Military Occupational Specialty, was 11B3V and he had earned the Ranger Tab. He was deployed in Helmand province in Afghanistan. Actions there earned Sgt/ Dickle a Bronze Star and a Purple Heart, he was given...."

"Wait a minute," Lottie said. "Purple Heart? He was wounded?"

"Yes. A bullet almost broke his left arm."

"How does a bullet almost break your arm?"

"It passed between the bones of his arm --- the radius and the ulna. He had to wear a cast and a sling for a few weeks."

"He never wrote us about it," Maude said. "And Ramona didn't mention it."

"His wife. No, he wouldn't," Lydecker said.

"Why not?" Lottie asked.

"This note from his commanding officer says he asked not to have it included in reports. Seems it was the kind of man he was. Which may be one of the reasons he was given a field commission --- as a second lieutenant."

"Jarvis was an officer?" Maude said looking ad Lottie.

"This is the first I've ever heard about it."

"You didn't know him at all."

"He never communicated with us, did he Lottie?"

"Not to me --- but then I was just his daughter."

"He didn't seem to do much better with Ramona. I know that 'cause she was living here with me."

"And they used the Internet," Lottie added.

"Lt. Dickle," the retired major said after a few moments studying the file, "was a platoon leader. His last in country assignment was to a two story house in the middle of nowhere. He had two sniper teams, two shooters and two spotters. The Lt. took his own M82 --- the Remington 700 rifle with scope. He wasn't supposed to be a shooter any more since he was an officer. The two teams both had .50 caliber M107."

"Is that important?" Maude asked.

"The ammo is different, ma'am. The Lt.'s rifle used N.A.T.O. 7.62 and the 107s the teams used were .50 caliber."

"So?" Lottie asked.

"They were stormed from all three sides by the Taliban. Our guys held them off --- for a while. Then the L.T. radioed in for more ammo. They helicoptered in two cases of .50 cal and one of 7.62. The problem was that the load was so heavy that it fell through the mud roof. By that point, one of the shooters and one of the spotters were already down."

"Wounded?"

"The spotter was killed and the sniper wounded. That's when the Lt. hauled the shooter downstairs on his back. Dickle patched up the wounded man up and loaded up with ammo which he took back to the two shooters up top --- the spotter of the wounded sniper took over the 107 and stayed in the fight. Lt. Dickle crawled from one side of the roof to the other delivering the ammo. He pulled one of the shooters aside as the first mortar hit. The sniper was able to find another position and carry on the fight while the Lt. supplied the other spotter turned shooter. Lt. Dickle was wounded twice more by this point and was bleeding but he kept moving. He also took up his rifle and went to work defending their position.

"When they started to run low again, Lt. Dickle headed back down when the second mortar hit. The whole side of the house caved in covering up both the wounded sniper and Lt. Dickle. That's when the third and fourth shells hit. The two men on the roof were killed in the barrage and both the Lt. and the spotter were trapped in the rubble.

"The report says the Taliban rushed the house just as two air support Worthogs, A-10 Thunderbolts, caught the majority of the opposition forces out in the open --- and tore hell out of them. The rest of the Lt.'s company arrived and the battle quickly shifted. The Taliban ran as they always do.

"It was a few hours later that they found the wounded sniper and Lt. Dickle. Both were med evaced out. Before the sniper died he dictated a statement of Lt. Dickle's action. He died not knowing that the L.T. was given the Silver Star."

"Silver Star?" Maude said in astonishment.

"Isn't that right under the Congressional Medal of Honor?" Lottie asked.

"Yes, ma'am," Lydecker said. "The C.O. wanted to make it the CMH --- but the Lt. refused to accept it. "Not from this President," he is reported to have said. His C.O. ordered him to accept the Silver Star --- on behalf of the men who were lost if nothing else --- or go to the brig. He did as he was told."

Caroline Montoya who sat beside Maude had her mouth open in surprise.

"Well, I will be damned for sure."

"How come we never knew anything about any of this?" Lottie asked. "Shouldn't the family be notified?"

"Lt. Dickle didn't want anybody to know."

"Why the hell not?" Maude demanded. "This makes no sense to me. If Jarvis was a decorated hero --- why? Why?"

"We have it in a few men with us," Lydecker said.

"Are they mean to everyone --- just assholes --- and I ask that as Jarvis's mother?"

"Yes, ma'am. Some get past it --- some never do. It's called survivors guilt." #

11

Neither Lottie nor Maude recognized the members of the Texas Rebel Snipers at Jarvis' funeral. They all wore dress green uniforms with green berets and polished boots. Each man also had his metals pinned to his chest and were both shaved and sported military haircuts.

Six men carried the flag covered, pine box that Jarvis had specified in a letter to the funeral home years ago up to the gravesite. Major Lydecker marched in step at the rear of the squad. The new Baptist minister, the Reverend Robert Peña, delivered the bland, platitude laden graveside eulogy saying mostly that no one, not even his family, really knew Jarvis Dickle --- what else could he do?

There was a much bigger crowd in attendance than anyone expected. The entire VFW seemed to have shown up as well as some people who everybody knew wouldn't piss on Jarvis if he were on fire. This was all thanks to an early morning editorial Roman Southworth had written for the newspaper and which Webb Fritz had read on the air. It was all based on what Lottie had told him she had learned about Jarvis --- a man no one in town really knew.

On command from the Sgt. Major, fifty yards away, seven men lifted their rifles and fired a military salute into the air. In the distance a trumpet player, also a member of the TRS played taps. After the flag was smartly folded into a triangle, it was handed to Major Lydecker who accepted it and the slow but erect salute from the last man in the detail. Lydecker delivered the flag on bended knee to Maude saying, "On behalf of a grateful nation and the United States Army, this flag is offered to you as a token of appreciation for your son's honorable and faithful service."

Lottie and Maude were brought to tears by the service; especially the filing past the casket by the members of the TRS, their laying a coin on the surface, stepping back and snapping a salute before marching away.

BACK AT MAUDE'S HOUSE, after those who felt obligated to come by and say something had left, Asa Hunt stood on the front porch talking with Lydecker when Lottie joined them.

"Ms. Truett, " Lydecker said removing his beret.

"Lottie," the sheriff greeted her taking off his straw hat.

"I want to thank you, Major, for the service today --- and for everything else," she looked at the fresh paint and the flag pole. "But most of all for telling us about my father. You were right --- we didn't know him at all."

"Not unusual, ma'am. We've seen it more times than you'd think."

"What were those coins your men left on the casket?"

"Unit coins. Some people call them challenge coins. They're the commemorative tokens of the campaign and outfits each man served with. If someone slaps one down on a bar, you have to buy his drinks all night unless you have a coin that out ranks his. One of the men hasn't bought drinks in years. His unit has over twenty-one Presidential Unit citations. Hard to beat."

"They put down their only coins?"

"No. Each of us has a stash of them. But we do leave one each time we do this."

"Can you tell me a little more about this survivor's guilt thing?" Lottie asked. "I don't watch enough daytime TV to be up on it."

"It's a form of P.T.S.D.," Asa said.

"After surviving a major traumatic event --- like the fire fight your father was in," Lydecker said, "and being the only or even one of the few who lived through it --- these people don't think they should be living when someone or the rest of their outfit didn't --- they're alive but they're not really living any more. They punish themselves and any joy they experience only makes them feel worse."

"As sheriff, I've seen it with accident and fire victims, too. People who have never been to war."

"They can't sleep well --- they have nightmares and flashbacks."

"The thing that stood out about Jarvis," the sheriff said, "was his inability to get along with folks. It started with you and your grand-mother cause you were the closest to him."

"There is a numb, detached feeling they have all the time." Lydecker said, "--- because they're living with constant intense fear and anxiety. They have heart issues, headaches, stomach aches, dizzi-ness --- suicidal thoughts. Basically Jarvis felt helpless and out of control. If he wasn't talking to anyone --- no one would know any of this."

"We all did see how easily Jarvis was irritated and agitated. The fact that he kept to himself so much was part of his unwillingness --- or inability --- to discuss the event or how he was feeling."

"That was Daddy."

"This is something that happened a long time ago, but you know who Buddy Holly was from going to school at Tech in Lubbock," Asa said.

"Sure. Big black horn rimed glasses --- rock'n roll star."

"You know how he was killed?"

"Plane crash?"

"Right. What you may not know is that Waylon Jennings was a guitarist for Buddy Holly. He had a seat on that private plane that night. But Waylon gave up his seat to another singer you probably never heard of, 'The Big Bopper'."

"I do know Waylon Jennings," Lottie said.

"Well, he was joking with Buddy Holly when he gave up his seat to The Big Bopper. Holly said something like, 'I hope your ol' bus freezes up.' And Waylon shot back with, 'Well, I hope your plane crashes.'"

"That must have been terrible when it did happen."

"Yeah, Waylon became a big country star --- but unless he got some help, those words must have haunted him for the rest of his life."

"When you soldier with somebody, putting your life on the line, covering his back and knowing he's covering yours ---," Lydecker said, "it's hard for civilians to understand but sometime those bonds, the things that make your unit a band of brothers can be stronger than any other feelings you ever know."

"We certainly didn't know anything about it," Lottie said.

"Have you even been over to your daddy's trailer?" Asa asked.

"No," Lottie admitted.

The sheriff fished out a set of keys from his pocket and handed them to Lottie.

"Keys to his truck and to his trailer. We've been over it looking for evidence. We didn't find anything useful. But you and Maude might."

Maude joined them on the porch.

"Major, thank you and your men for everything."

"Wish we could say it was a pleasure, ma'am. But it was a duty and an honor."

"Words I never expected to hear about my son. It makes me humble and damn sorry for not being a better mother to him."

"If you don't mind my sayin' so," Asa said, "you did a damn fine job raising Jarvis. The way he turned out --- the very best of it --- was 'cause of you, Maude. The worst of it had more to do with the war than anything else."

"In the end --- Jarvis will be remembered as an ass," Asa said, "Could be that's what he wanted. And for whatever it means, I think he was loved by the mules he worked with."

Maude made a face at that remark. "Who cares?"

"Maybe Daddy did," Lottie said.

"Asses to asses," Maude said. #

12

Dallas didn't fly the next morning --- too windy --- all his work would be blown away before it got down to the crops. It's the nature of cropdusting. Instead he went with Lottie and Maude to Jarvis' trailer. The park, if you could call it that, was an acre and a half of concrete pads with water, sewer, and electrical hook ups, named The OK Corral.

A tree had died a couple of years before beside Jarvis' short adobe and rust colored single wide. In a former life it had perhaps been a food wagon for Mexican or Asian cruisine. It was up on blocks but a glance at the tires would tell you that they were all cracked and most likely devoid of air. A bent TV antenna clung to the flat roof in desperation. This was the kind of place that attracted if not spawned tornadoes.

The interior matched the exterior --- not just in drab colors but with a lack of attention. The place wasn't dirty but the couch had a hole in one arm covered by a pillow. A small screen black and white TV was wedged onto the lip between the front window and the door. The place smelled of both mold and dry rot. A small cactus was trying to die on the sill over the sink.

"You ever been here?" Maude asked Lottie.

"I stopped outside once. Daddy wasn't home so I left. I forget what I was mad at him about."

There was half a six pack of Shiner beer in the fridge and two frozen solid TV dinners.

The bath was a fiberglass shower and a toilet with the seat up. The stains of both were difficult to distinguish between biological, rust, and water deposits.

There was a knock on the front door. Dallas answered it.

"Tomas Duran." the beer bellied, 40's, dark receding hair said. "I'm the manager. You folks must be Jarvis' kin."

"They are," Dallas said nodding toward Maude and Lottie. "I'm just along for the fun of it."

"Well, I just wanted to tell you that Jarvis is paid up to the end of the year. The trailer can stay here that long. After that you'll need to move it or sell it."

"Somebody wants to buy it?" Maude asked from behind Dallas.

"Not at the moment. But somebody will come along. If nothing else I might give you what it would cost to move it and have the scrap yard take it."

"Don't be in a rush. I might decide to make this my summer home."

"You're kiddin'," Duran said.

"Of course she's kidding," Dallas said. "We'll let you know."

Dallas started to close the door when Duran stopped him.

"Here is Jarvis' mail. It comes to the main office."

Dallas took the mail and closed the door.

The bed wasn't made and the sheets were long past the need of a washing. Only a good fire could fix them. Under the mattress and box springs was where Jarvis's treasures hid. They consisted of a collection of four handguns, two rifles with scopes, and a .12 gauge pump shotgun. There was also a box for each of the metals Jarvis had been awarded in the service, including his gold 2nd lieutenant bars. A stack of DD-214 discharge papers was on top of the orders for his awards and promotion.

"Asa must have seen all this," Lottie said looking through the pages. "How come he never let on."

"I think he wanted us to find these for ourselves, Nana."

Maude studied the Silver Star a moment. "I don't mind his not telling us about all this --- but he should have told Ramona. She died not knowing he was a hero."

"From what the major and Asa told me last night, Daddy never thought of himself as a hero. He was ashamed of all this. Why would he want to share it with his wife?"

"Cause she was dying and he knew he wasn't going to be there for her."

"Part of this I don't think we'll ever understand. I do feel better knowing why he was so angry all the time --- and I'm sorry I didn't treat him any better."

Dallas pulled Lottie to him.

"He didn't want you to know or he'd have told you, Lottie. This ---," Dallas swept his hand to the trailer, "his whole life --- it was his hell and he tried to keep those he loved from being any part of it. I get that."

"Well, I don't," Maude said snapping the velvet box shut. "If he wanted to be left alone, okay. I'd --- we'd all have left him alone. But not knowing why --- that's the terrible part of it. Hell, look at the people we put up with everyday who are a pain in the ass but we just say, 'God bless 'em' and go on."

"I believe Daddy thought God had cursed him."

They looked around the closet and in the cupboards and found nothing else.

"Dallas," Maude said finally, "you interested in any of those guns?"

"Not really. This the .12 Jarvis used to shoot Lottie's ex?"

"I expect so."

"I'm not interested. I could clean 'em and give 'em back to you --- but it they look to be in good shape. You hang on to them," he said. "Maybe in a year of so you might want to do something else with them."

"Like what?"

"Give'em away --- let the sheriff have'em."

"Good enough."

Lottie stood at the sink looking at the cactus.

"Why would Daddy have a cactus? He didn't have any plants outside."

"Well, none that are alive," Maude said.

"So why one inside. And why a cactus?"

"Nobody's going to touch it," Dallas said.

"Who did he ever have over for a visit?" Maude frowned.

Lottie picked up the little plant and found a fork in the drawer and poked around in the dirt. The fork hit something. She dug it out. It was a small oddly shaped key.

"One-hundred-sixty-two," she read.

She handed the key to Maude who looked it over and handed it to Dallas.

"It's a safety deposit box key," Dallas said.

"How do you know that?" Lottie asked.

Dallas pulled out his key ring and showed them a key that looked very similar.

"What are you doing with a safety deposit box?" Lottie wanted to know.

"That where I keep my flight log books and the papers for the plane --- and a ring that belonged to my grandmother I'd like somebody special to wear --- but she keeps putting me off. You should have been a detective," Dallas said.

"What bank?"

"Mine's with Texas State Bank. This looks like the exact same kind."

"There's no Texas State Bank in town --- or anywhere close that I know of?"

"Plainview," Dallas said. "That's the nearest. It's where my box is."

"Let's pack up the guns and Jarvis's military stuff. We're having lunch in Plainview."

"We can go eat there but the banks closed. Sunday."

"We still need to eat." Looking at her watch Maude said, "The Catholics are out and there'll be a line at Leal's. We'd have to get a move on to even get a seat at Mom's. The Baptist are wrapping up right now."

"We're goin' to end up at the Coffee Mug," Dallas said.#

13

"We can save some time," Maude told Inez Brinkley while Lottie and Dallas looked at the menus. "You tell me what you know, and I'll fill in the gaps with anything I think is any of your damn business."

"Don't be that way, Mother Dickle," the chief gossip in Muleshoe said. Inez was wide hipped and so heavy everyone expected if she ever tipped over, she'd land in their soup or coffee. "This is a small town and people care about you. We know what a terrible tragedy you've been through."

"And since they moved Jerry Springer to late nights, there's not enough on The View, Ellen, and Dr. Phil to keep everybody entertained."

"We know you went to Jarvis' trailer today. Did you find his medals? You know the VFW is talkin' about renaming their post after your son."

"Since he never darkened their door, I'm sure he'd be proud. What's the special today?"

"Turkey and dressing dinner," Inez said.

Lottie and Dallas put down their menus and nodded. Maude collected the laminated sheets and handed them back to Inez.

"Three specials with iced tea."

"All right," Inez scribble on her pad. "Pumpkin pie for dessert? It's fresh."

"Yep," Maude said.

Inez walked toward the counter and the kitchen pass-through calling, "Three specials with pumpkin pie!"

"Fresh out of the can," Maude said to Lottie.

"I heard that," Inez said.

"I'd only be surprised if you didn't."

ASA HUNT SPENT Sunday afternoon going over all reports and photographs from the crime scene. The only thing explainable was the thin trail of pressed down weeds from the back of Jarvis' shop out to the side road which lead back to the highway, U.S. 70 and 84.

The sheriff picked up his desk phone as he pulled out the leaf with his list of important phone numbers taped to it. He had to put his bifocals on to read and punch in the numbers. After a moment Sheriff Martin Ybarra of Curry County, New Mexico, answered.

"Asa? What in Curry County can I do for you?"

Asa could picture the handsome mid-thirties Sheriff in a plaid shirt of some sort driving along in his official patrol SUV using his vehicle cell phone.

"I'd like to come over to your backyard tomorrow and talk to the only witness I have on the Jarvis Dickle murder."

"Hazen Snead? He a suspect?"

"Nope. But still the only witness I have --- and he wasn't even there when it happened."

"Sounds like you're graspin' at sand burrs."

"More like dust devils. There's just simply no physical evidence in this."

"And you think Hazen could help?"

"Oh, hell, Martin, I don't know if anybody can help."

"Come ahead. You're not steppin' on my toes."

"I'd like you to come with me, if you've got the time."

"You want to use my gas instead of yours?"

Asa laughed.

"Naw. More like I'd liked to have somebody's else eyes and ears on this. I'm feelin' old. There's got to be something I'm missin', but I don't see it."

"Sure thing," Sheriff Yabarra said. "When?"

"How's eight-thirty sound?"

"See you here."

Asa hung up and called Hazen Snead the Clovis area rancher who had brought his mules to Jarvis the day the mule farrier was found dead.

"You going to be around your place tomorrow, Hazen?" Asa asked when the witness picked up.

"I'm still tryin' t' make this place turn a profit. I'll be here. What's up?"

"I'd like to ask you some questions about the day Jarvis was killed."

"Okay, but I don't know any more now than I did that day."

"Sometimes it's a matter of my askin' the right question."

"You're goin' to be comin' a long way to hear the same answers."

"Most likely," Asa said. "We'll be there a little after nine."

"We? You got a rabbit in your pocket?"

"Martin Yabarra is coming, too. I'm out of my jurisdiction. It's a matter of courtesy."

"I can tell him the same things I told you."

"ONE THING I noticed wasn't in the trailer," Dallas said sitting back and pushing away the canned pumpkin pie. "A will. Do you think Jarvis ever made one?"

"If he thought it would make it harder on us, he most likely didn't," Maude said.

"Nana, you've got to stop being s' hard on Daddy. He was dealing with a lot of demons." Lottie was thumbing through the mail the mobile home park manager had handed Travis. It was mostly junk mail.

"Oh, honey, I know. I just can't get the picture of Jarvis out of my head that he took years to paint. I think part of it is that I still don't forgive him for not being there for your mother. Ramona deserved better than that."

"What little I remember," Lottie said, "now makes we think their marriage was over before he went off that last time. Momma said something about Daddy's insurance was only good as long as they were married. And he didn't want that to stop for her --- being sick."

"She tried like hell to make things work."

Lottie stopped and pulled out one white envelope and looked closely at the return address.

"Was Daddy on disability?"

"Should have been with those purple hearts," Dallas said.

"It's news to me," Maude said.

Lottie ran a finger under the edge of the flap and ripped the top of it open. She extracted a check from the U.S. Department of Veteran's Affairs. She was surprised at the amount and handed the check to her grandmother.

"Where would Jarvis be cashing these?" she wondered.

"What's the story on Jarvis and the other tours?" Dallas asked. "Was he PTSD from just that last tour?"

"He never talked about it," Maude said, giving up on her pie too. "It was like it never happened --- at least as far as his sharing it."

"Maybe his not saying anything was the first sign," Lottie said. "Or the fact that he wasn't eating much."

Louder than she needed to, Maude said, "If Jarvis had pie like this, it could have put him off his feed for good."#

14

The next day was another windy, and this time rainy day, as the squalls coursed down the east side of the Rocky Mountains and on to the flat lands of New Mexico and the plains of West Texas. By 8:40 A.M. Asa Hunt had parked his Bailey County Sheriff's SUV in front of the Curry County, New Mexico, Sheriff's Office. The mid-thirties, handsome Sheriff of Curry County, Martin Ybarra, was waiting for him. They both hurriedly got in Sheriff Ybarra's vehicle not exchanging handshakes until they were out of the rain showers.

"You ever been out to Hazen Snead's place?" Ybarra asked.

"No. I don't even understand why he comes to my turf to get his mules worked on instead of having it taken care of around here."

"We can ask him."

The Snead Ranch was farm and ranch magazine pretty. All the fence posts were painted along the muddy road which had been recently graded up to the main house.

The two sheriffs met the rancher in his barn where he was dry but having worked up a good sweat from his labors. He was a little over 5 ft. 10 and all muscle and sinew.

"Dueling sheriffs. Makes me wish I played the banjo."

"Hazen," Asa said.

"Mr. Snead," Sheriff Ybarra nodded.

"Seems like I get more respect here at home than I do over in Texas."

"You also vote here," Asa said.

"True," Hazen laughed. "Let's pull up a couple of bales. I don't spend a lot of my time riding around in air conditioned comfort."

As they all sat, it was the New Mexico sheriff who had the first question.

"Why did you take your business across the state line? We've got mule farriers here."

"I was at the county fair several years back showing off a couple of my mules. I heard Jarvis arguing with somebody. I heard him say, 'All a mule has is its life! And he or she works for a living every day! They can't reproduce --- they leave nothing behind! I'd horsewhip any man who'd mistreat a mule!'

"I knew then he was the man to take care of my animals. Don't get me wrong --- I didn't like Jarvis any better than anybody else. But he was, hands down, the best mule farrier around. We'd do business but we didn't talk."

"You given any more thought to that day when we found Jarvis dead?" Asa asked.

"Not a whole lot. I told you what I knew. I dropped my mules off in his holding yard before he even opened up. The first I heard about his been killed was on the radio at the Coffee Mug. I drove back out there, talked to you, Sheriff, picked up my mules and came home."

"You ever go around back of his shop?"

"Nope. I saw he wasn't open so I backed my trailer up to his gate and got ol' Barney and Bess out. Locked up the gate and drove into town to have breakfast."

"What do you remember about the trip over?" Sheriff Ybarra asked. "Anything stick out in your memory."

Hazen thought for a moment before he said, "It was raining --- not as hard as now, but enough to make the roads slick and make me use my wipers."

"Much traffic then?"

"Never is. Oh, there was this one jackass on a motor bike who almost got himself killed."

"How's that?" Asa pressed.

"Well, he didn't have any wipers --- stupid to be out riding in that kind of weather on those stupid English saddle racing bikes."

"English saddle?"

"Yeah. Not like a Harley where you ride with your legs down or even out in front like you're on a bronc. This was one of those where you lean forward and curl your legs up behind you."

"And how did he almost get killed?"

"I don't think he could see all that well through that dark helmet. He pulled out from behind me and darted back just before a semi damn near made a cow paddy out of him. I had to hit my brakes and almost jackknifed b'fore he sped on off --- weaving a little like he wasn't all that good a rider to begin with."

"What color was the bike," Asa asked.

"Lime green. Japanese --- I don't remember which brand but I knew it wasn't American."

As the two lawmen were about to make the run back to Sheriff Ybarra's SUV, Hazen Snead had one last thought.

"Is that story true about Jarvis shooting Tagg Truett in the ass with a .12 gauge?"

"Yep," Asa said. "Why?"

"Oh, it just came to mind the other day when I saw Tagg in Billy The Kid's."

Asa shot a questioning look at Martin Ybarra.

"Local cowboy titty bar down on South Highway 70."

"Thanks, Hazen."

"I actually helped? Don't know I intended to do that."

"Think of it as doing something for your mules," Asa said.

"Yeah. I could do that."

∼

DALLAS DIDN'T GO FLYING that day either. Instead, he was with Lottie and Maude in his candy apple red, extended cab Chevy Silverado long bed. They were driving the sixty miles due east to check out the Texas State Bank in Plainview. Maude sat in the back seat and Lottie rode shotgun.

"Caroline says she got back on her computer and there were messages from several of the kids who grew up at our place. They couldn't pick up the telephone, but they can run on and on with that damn Facebook," Maude said.

"That's the way the younger generation is," Lottie said. "They'd rather text than talk. I'm surprised you didn't get a bunch of text messages on your phone."

"I might have but I'd never know it." She looked from her grand-daughter to Dallas. "You two text each other?"

"Sure," Lottie said. "Some of the things we text to each other you don't want to know about, Nana."

"Oh, I get it. Sex texting. That what you call it?"

"Sexting," Lottie laughed.

"Well, don't do any of it while we're driving, okay?"

Dallas and Lottie laughed.

"Look here," Maude went on, "you made me get a cell phone so if I have a stroke I can call 911. I even talk to people on it. But I ain't going to try to thumb my way through keys too small for me to see much less type on. Somebody has something to say t' me they can damn sure call and say it or leave me the hell alone."

Just then Maude's cell phone started to ring.

"Up pops the devil," she said digging the small device out of purse. She clicked it on and said into it, "Whatever you're sellin', I ain't buyin'. S' don't waste your time or mine."

Maude listened for a few moments and looked over at Lottie in the front seat with a curious expression.

"I never heard of you," Maude said into the phone. After a pause she spoke again. "I was just his mother. That didn't mean he talked to me." Another pause. "Amarillo. Well, as it turns out, I'm on my way to Plainview. Wait a minute." Then to Dallas she said, "You think we might be able to drive up to Amarillo this afternoon if this bank business doesn't take too long?"

"Not a problem," Dallas said.

Back into the phone Maude said, "How do I get hold of you once I'm there?"

Maude listened a few moments and then handed the phone over to Lottie.

"Here you talk to this, guy."

Lottie took the phone and pressed it up to her ear and said, "Hello. Lottie Truett." She paused before saying, "Yes, I am."

For several moments Lottie just listened as they drove. Finally she said, "Okay, Mr. Creighton. I'll call you when we're about there. Good bye."

She gave the phone back to her grandmother.

To Dallas she said, "Looks like Daddy did have a will. That's his lawyer we need to go to see today."

"This is turning into a real adventure," Dallas said with a wink. "We've got the truck for it."

"I started to say," Maude said looking around inside from the back seat, "this is the most comfortable truck I think I've ever been in."

"Don't get him started," Lottie warned.

"My art, my pride and joy," Dallas said reaching over and patting Lottie's knee, "--- after you, of course."

"Don't believe it. He'd rather spend time in his second hanger working on his toys than playing with his band."

"A hell of a toy," Maude said.

"Notice how much room you have? I chopped six inches off the bed and extended the cab by that much. Those seats are front seats and they have space to recline. And check out the window."

Maude looked at the rectangle window beside her.

"What about it?"

"It's not the original equipment window. It's an Airstream trailer window."

"Looks like it belongs."

"That's the point. Seamless."

"Where did you learn to do all this?"

"The Internet. You can learn anything you want on the Internet."

"Even things you know how to do," Lottie said with a wink putting her hand on one of Dallas's knees, "--- you can learn to do better?"

"I don't believe I want to know this," Maude said.

They all laughed.#

15

The bank manager, a pleasant woman in her 50s with hair which looked as if it were growing back from chemotherapy took the key from Maude and checked her computer.

"Do you have some identification?"

Maude show her driver's license and so did Lottie. The woman returned Maude's license but to Lottie she said, "We've been expecting you."

This surprised Lottie, Maude, and Dallas.

To Maude the lady said, "Mrs. Dickle, the box is in your granddaughter's name and in the name of Mr. Dickle."

"Guess he figured to outlive me. I would have thought the same thing," Maude said putting her license away.

"Do you have a death certificate?"

Maude produced one.

"May we keep this for our files?"

"Oh, yeah," Maude said. "The funeral home gave us a stack."

"Before I show you to the box, do you have a disability check you'd like to cash?"

Lottie pulled this item from her purse.

"Was this a kind of routine with --- my father?"

"Yes. Each month he'd come in, cash his check, and then go to his safety deposit box."

The lady got Lottie to sign the check in Jarvis's name and add, "by Lottie Dickle Truette." She took the check to the nearest cashier, got the check cashed and returned with the money in an envelope.

"If you'll follow me now."

Inside the vault the manager inserted one key and Lottie the other one. The manager opened the box and removed both keys handing Lottie one back.

"Please let me know when you're ready to close up."

The lady left the vault.

Lottie tried to pull out the make-up case sized box behind the double locked doors but seemed to be struggling with it when Dallas stepped over and helped her remove the box and set it down on the waist high table in the middle of the walls lined with other safety deposit boxes.

Flipping a latch, Lottie opened the lid to discover a box filled with cash. It was mostly hundred dollar bills bundled together with a paper band. The box was well over three quarters full.

"Seriously," Dallas said, "will you marry me, Lottie?"

They left the box in the Plainview bank with the addition of the envelope of Jarvis's cashed disability check. They had hardly said a word as they roughly counted the treasure, then closed it back up and called the manager to relock the box back into its slot.

Almost twenty minutes later as they headed north on Interstate 27 to Amarillo, Maude broke the silence.

"That's more than just his disability for the last fifteen years."

"Hazen Snead told Asa that Daddy did all his business in cash," Lottie said.

"But even together --- all of it --- unless he never spent a dime and put it all in that box...," Dallas said unable to finish the thought.

"We saw the palace he was living in," Maude said. "You've seen his ol' truck. He dressed like a hobo. He didn't eat much. What else did he spend his money on? It wasn't women and song."

They drove on and finally Maude said, "You might as well open the letter and read it."

Inside the safety deposit box, on the top of the money had been a sealed envelope addressed to Lottie. She had picked it up and looked at it, but she couldn't bring herself to open it. Now, miles up the road there seemed nothing else to do.

Dallas pulled a pocket knife out of his jeans and handed it to Lottie sensing that she didn't want to rip it open. She pried the blade out and slit the long edge under the flap. A single piece of paper was inside, hand written, these were the words of Jarvis Dickle. She unfolded the triple folded sheet and looked over it for a few moments before she began to read out loud.

"*Lottie, girl: if you're reading this, I'm gone. I'm sorry for --- for every-thing. My life, what I did to your mother, your grandmother --- to you. I hurt the women in my life more than any of them ever deserved. I know saying I'm sorry doesn't make up for it. I don't know anything I could ever do to make up for it.*

"*By now maybe you've figured out what it was made me like I am. But I can't blame it on the war. I can only blame my life on me. I'm the one who wouldn't or couldn't let things go. I'm the one who let things kink me up to where I was no good to anyone. At least I was always good to mules. At least I tried to be.*

"*My mother raised me better than that. My wife loved me enough to put up with me and tried her best to give me time and space to deal with things, but none of it was enough. And then there was you. You, too young to understand any of it and me being so hateful to everyone --- especially those closest to me. Anybody who reached out to me I gave them back spite, spit, and anger.*

"*What's in the box doesn't make up for it. I don't even mean for you to take it that way. This is all there was I had to give. I saved it up and kept it secret.*

"*I'm not asking you to forgive me. I don't know even God has enough forgiveness for me. I know I didn't earn it with my life. If God does forgive me – if you someday find a way to forgive me – it will be more than I ever deserve. If He can't – if you can't, there's nobody who would understand any better than me.*

"*I'd like to say, Love, Daddy – but I don't know how you could possibly believe it. Yet, it is true. I do – I always did – love you – your mother – and my own mother who broke her heart trying to make a better man out of me.*

"*I'm so sorry for who and what I was.*

"*Jarvis Dickle.*"

Dallas drove on in silence as Lottie and Maude both softly cried and mourned a man they never knew.#

16

Creighton, Leggett and Kelton, Attorneys At Law, was located on the 8th floor of the art deco Sante Fe Building on Polk Street downtown Amarillo. Built in 1930, the fourteen story building was for years the regional headquarters of the Atchison, Topeka and Sante Fe Railroad. For most of the 1990's the legal firm was one of only a few tenants in the grand structure until it was purchased by Potter County. Today it housed primarily County offices --- except for Creighton, Legget and Kelton.

The elegant if stodgy dark wood paneled offices could have been at home in a world where Victorian England collided with the American West. Lottie, Maude, and Dallas were ushered into the corner office of W. Leroy Creighton. The attorney, long past retirement age, offered a lively, somewhat boney, firm handshake. He had only a fringe of white hair remaining, but his dark eyes were clear and sharp through his rimless glasses. He wore a perfectly tailored pin stripped blue suit with a matching tie.

When everyone was seated, Creighton said, "It's my failure to contact you any earlier Ms. Truett, I apologize."

"It was not a problem," Lottie said. "We didn't know Daddy even had a will much less an attorney."

"As was his wish," the attorney said. "I believe that explains why he came to Amarillo to find a legal representation and have his will filed here instead of Bailey County."

"My son had more than his share of strange ways," Maude said. "Nothing about him surprises us anymore."

"I do want to express my condolences on Mr. Dickle's death."

"You know it was murder?" Maude asked.

"I do. I also know about the TRS rendering full military honors to your son. I was in attendance at his funeral, Mrs. Dickle, but chose not to make my presence known at that time."

"Is there some big mystery about Daddy's will or his estate?"

"No. But what little I knew of Lt. Dickle told me that he was a man who kept to himself, didn't want his business to be anybody else's --- and that he carried a heavy load from his days in combat."

"I think you knew more --- or at least understood more --- about my son than I did."

"In my time I have seen the ravages of war on the souls of way too many who have served our country when called upon and then forgotten when they returned with injuries --- seen and unseen."

Mr. Creighton opened a folder on his desk and unfolded a single piece of paper which even Lottie, Maude and Dallas could see was signed, witnessed and officially stamped.

"This is the official reading of the last will and testament of Jarvis Delmar Dickle. 'I, Jarvis Delmar Dickle being of sound mind and body hereby appoint Mr. W. Leroy Creighton as the executor of my will and estate.

"I bequeath all my worldly goods and possessions to my only heir and daughter, Lottie Ramona Dickle.

"My one codicil is that my working tools and gear in my work-shop I leave to the Panhandle-Plains Museum at West Texas A&M in the event they are interested in any of them. Otherwise, my shop and tools should be sold at auction and the proceeds given to my daughter, Lottie.

"After probate the proceeds from my enclosed life insurance policies, both military and civilian, are to go to my daughter as well."

Creighton looked up and said, "It is signed, witnessed, and notarized."

He held up two insurance policies.

"The policy from the Marine Corps has been converted into an Allstate policy for ten grand to cover the cost of burial. The other," he indicated the thicker of the two documents, "is a policy for $500,000.00. There is a double indemnity clause in the event of foul play --- murder. So it will cash out at an even one million dollars."

"My God," Lottie said as she sagged back in her chair. She looked over at Maude. There were tears in her eyes.

"For the first time in many years, I am proud of my son."

Lottie turned to Dallas who made no joke this time but just squeezed her hand lightly.

SHERIFF ASA HUNT spent the afternoon with his counter point, Sheriff Martin Ybarra, digging out the facts about Tagg Truett, Lottie's ex-husband. The thirty-six year old didn't have any kind of criminal record with the sole exception of a single DUI. He would have been a handsome man if he had employed his smile more. He had natural dimples in both cheeks but they only revealed themselves when he wasn't sulking, which was his predominate habit.

Clovis, besides being the county seat of New Mexico's Curry County, was the home to Cannon Air Force Base. Tagg had served there as an aircraft mechanic but was only promoted once during his nearly four years on the base. These days he was a bartender at Billy The Kid, what Sheriff Ybarra aptly called a cowboy titty bar. The single story adobe covered cinderblock building was just far enough away from the military post to not be within its authority.

Tagg shared a two bedroom apartment off of East 5th with a long haul truck driver named Coy Vanderveer. Like Tagg, Vanderveer was divorced but had a clean record. He didn't own his own rig but drove for Clovis Coast to Coast Trucking.

Tagg had no motorcycle and but his roommate did. It was a lime green Kawasaki. The questions were, where was the bike and did Tagg have any access to it?#

17

Lottie called Webb that night and told him she would be back to work in the morning and she planned to get back to normal A.S.A.P. The station owner and manager said he was glad to hear it, but to let him know if something came up and she needed more time off.

After she and Dallas had made love that night, he realized she was watching him long after they had both gotten their breath back.

"What?" he asked.

"Nothing," Lottie said.

"Which means 'something.' Out with it."

"I've been seriously considering your proposal," she told him after a pause.

"Well, there are now some strings attached."

"Like what."

"A prenup for one."

Lottie shot up in bed and turned on the light so she could see Dallas's eyes.

"What are you saying to me?"

"You are now a woman of property, Lottie," he said reaching for her hand which she pulled back. "Let's be realistic --- more than half of all marriages fail --- ours won't --- I promise that."

"But?" she asked her jaw tightening.

"But in the unforeseen event that it doesn't ---"

"Yes?" Lottie crossed her arms across her breasts.

"--- what belongs to you --- belongs to you and you alone. You've had a hard life with men --- especially your father. What he left you is more than money. It was his way of saying he loved you and really cared about you. Nobody, including me, has, or should have, any right to take any of that away from you. Not only wouldn't I do it --- I want it in writing ahead of time that there's no way I could."

Lottie dove into his arms and kissed him with passion and tears.

Before they could begin making love again, Dallas said, "That financial advisor your lawyer told you about --- I think she should be able to draw up something. We do that and I'll go back and get my grandmother's ring."

WHEN WEBB TOOK over the control room to read the noon news, Lottie found Asa Hunt waiting for her in the lobby.

"Sheriff Hunt," she said. "This is an official call, I take it?"

"Could we have lunch somewhere, Lottie? I need to ask you a few more questions."

"As long as we don't go to the Coffee Mug."

"I was thinking Leal's."

"You're on."

TEX-MEX FOOD DOESN'T GET any better than it does at Leal's. The family owned business which started in Muleshoe had expanded into Clovis, Plainview, Amarillo, and Lubbock. For those who have eaten there they say it's the best definition of blends of Texas and Mexican cuisine.

"Sorry to do this to you, Lottie, but --- "

"Don't worry about it, Sheriff. Nothing can put me in a bad mood today."

"Even talking about Tagg Truett?"

Lottie sighed, finished chewing and took a swallow of ice tea before she said, "Not even that. What do you want to know?"

"How would you describe him?"

"He thinks he's God's gift to women. Those dimples are the thing. When he flashes them --- things happen to girls between their legs they don't want to confess. He should have stayed in the Air Force. He filled out his uniform in all the right places. But Tagg doesn't have any ambition or drive. He wants to live off his looks --- and his ability to catch a football and run with it. The football thing played out after high school. He wasn't willing to work at even that hard enough to get a football scholarship --- so it was the service for him. He's had any girl he wanted since high school --- but that was as good as it got for him. He's been on a downhill slide ever since."

"Why did you marry him?"

"Those dimples --- and we both thought I was pregnant. I wasn't. Once he found that out the marriage thing was in-name-only for him --- and a convenient lay. He was chasing every skirt or tight fitting pair of jeans between here and Clovis. I knew it --- but over looked it a few times --- then I realized I had become a laughing stock. I changed the locks on the doors, but he broke in one night anyway.

"You read all the police reports."

"I have. But I wanted to hear it from you."

"Well, he didn't rape me, which is what everybody thinks. He wanted to, but I had my .9 millimeter and knew how to use it --- and he knew it. When I pulled it out of the drawer, Tagg backed off. I want in the bedroom, locked the door and put a chair under the knob."

Lottie remembered that night so long ago.

"I went to bed after a while --- it sounded like he was getting beers out of the ice box and drinking. Finally I laid down on the bed, with the pistol still in my hand --- he woke me up when he slammed the front door and squealed out in that damn truck of his."

"And the next time you saw him?"

"He was in the emergency room claiming Daddy tried to kill him." Lottie remembered the night and took a deep breath, another swallow of tea and picked up her last taco. "If Daddy had wanted to kill Tagg, he'd done more than blow a chunk out of his butt."

"Why didn't he press charges against Jarvis?"

"He was ashamed, I think."

"And you never saw Jarvis that night?"

"Not then and not for --- oh --- a couple of months. Even that was out on the highway. He was driving one way and I was headed the other. We didn't wave."

Asa thought about what Lottie had told him for a bit before he asked, "Tagg moved out as soon as he got out of the hospital?"

"He did. I helped him pack his pickup. He wasn't moving too well or too fast."

"You filed for divorce?" Lottie nodded to the Sheriff's question.

"He had an apartment in Clovis by then. I'll bet it's the same place where he's still living."

Lottie finished her meal and so did Asa.

"You're askin' me all this 'cause you think it was Tagg that murdered Daddy?"

"It's a possibility."

"Like they say on the cop shows, I'd say he had 'motive.' Now, as for 'means and opportunity' --- I don't know. And why now? Daddy shot him years ago. You'd think he'd gotten over it by now."

"You'd think."

After lunch, Lottie decided to spend an hour out on her Nana's ranch shooting at rusted cans on the fence with her pistol. Just the thought about Tagg brought up memories and anger she'd thought she'd dealt with. Turns out, she hadn't.#

18

F isher Minard sat in an interview room in the Bailey County Sheriff's Office. Sheriff Asa Hunt had only one of his deputies, Polly Clover, on his side of the table. The young black women with buzz cut hair and circle silver earrings was as keen a detective as she was an attractive deputy.

"Do I need a lawyer?" Fisher asked looking around the stark room.

"Not unless you've done something wrong," Deputy Clover said.

"Everybody's done *something* wrong," the barrel chested, average height package delivery driver said. "And we've all thought about things we shouldn't --- but you can't arrest a guy for what he's thinking, now can you?"

"Sometime the problem is your keeping your thoughts to yourself," she winked. "What you don't know is that somebody else might be thinking the same thing you are."

"Oh, I doubt that," he grinned. "Not the kind of thoughts I have."

"Well, it's not what you think about that gets you in trouble as much as which thoughts you act on," she smirked just a little.

"If everybody had a record like yours, Fisher, we'd be out of a job around here," Asa said and his deputy smiled.

Fisher returned the smile and said. "I'm no saint. You have to know that, too." His brown eyes were about the same color as his driver's uniform but his eyes were a little mischievous.

"The major thing we want," Deputy Clover said in a kind voice, "is to merely ask you to go over the events of the morning you discovered Jarvis Dickle's body."

"I told you everything I knew that morning. Several times. To almost everyone there."

"We don't doubt it, Fisher, but we need to make sure we didn't miss something by not asking the right questions."

The major feature of the young man was that he had no ear lobes. He was an average guy in every respect but not threatening either.

"Can you tell us your story once more?"

"I feel like I've memorized this speech."

"Just one more time?" Asa asked.

"Okay, here goes.

"I had just made my first delivery of the day to Dave's Custom Auto --- he's usually my first delivery. He's on the other end of that building from where Jarvis is. It was six to eight boxes --- I remember two of them were front fenders for a '96 Mustang. The rest were all smaller boxes. Dave had on ear protectors 'cause he was still sanding on the back panel of the that Mustang. Anyway, I unloaded all the boxes inside his bay before I walked around and waved my arms to get his attention. He saw me, shut off the sander, took off his ear muffs and put in his hearing aids. We said "Hi" and he checked the boxes and signed the receipts. I gave him his copy and went back to the truck.

"I took a long swing around the parking lot to head out when I noticed somebody laying on the floor in Jarvis's place."

"Do you ever deliver anything to Jarvis?" Asa asked.

"Never have. The only way I knew his name wasn't by the sign outside his shop --- he didn't have one --- but Dave had told me what a S.O.B. he was. I was glad never to have had to deal with him."

"Was it still raining when you got out of the truck?"

"Yup. It had actually let up a tad since I had unloaded the boxes for Dave. I knew it was winding down."

"Go ahead," the sheriff said.

"I stopped, put the truck in park at the end of my turn. I looked back to make sure I was seeing what I thought and I was sure. I trotted over and there was Jarvis dead on the floor. I've seen enough TV to know that everything is evidence --- so I backed out trying to use the same wet shoe prints I'd made coming in. I pulled out my phone and called 911.

"Then I shut off my motor 'cause I knew I was going to be there a while and they teach us not to waste gas."

"Were there any mules in the gated yard beside the shop?"

"Two. But that's about all I can tell you about them."

"Okay."

"So I stayed in the truck until you arrived, Deputy Clover," Fisher said to Polly.

"I remember," she said checking her notes. "And you saw or heard nothing while you waited?"

"Not a thing. Well, I turned on the radio but other than that, no, not a thing."

"Could you close your eyes a moment?" Polly asked.

"Yes. Please," Asa asked, too.

"What the hell?" Fisher said and closed his eyes.

The deputy took over the questioning.

"Remember that day --- the rain --- it was letting up --- you were turning your truck around on the pavement of the parking lot. Something caught your eye and you saw Jarvis Dickle dead on the floor of his shop. Think back. What was it that caught your eye?"

"I don't know --- Jarvis laying there."

"Your attention --- your eyes --- are usually drawn to light or motion. Did you see light? Both bay doors of Jarvis' shop were open. Was there a light inside? Or outside?"

"Nope. I saw his furnace was on when I went inside, but I didn't see that from the truck."

"But back in your truck, you were paying attention to where the pavement ran out and turning your truck around without getting in the grass and the mud. What caused you to look in Jarvis' shop?"

Fisher Minard scrunched up his face as he tried to remember. Then his expression froze and his eyes opened.

"There was some motion. I don't know what it was, but something was moving on the far side of his shop. Something in that tall grass back there."

"Okay," Deputy Clover said carefully, "as you trotted over and saw Jarvis' body and as you made your way back to your truck --- looking down at your cell phone to call 911, did you hear anything? You were right there by the highway."

He thought a moment and then said, "A motorcycle."

"What kind. A big ol' hog? What?"

"No. It was more like one of those --- dirt bikes --- no --- a street bike One of those Japanese kinds you have to lean over on to ride."

"When you got back in your truck and waited for us to get there," Asa asked now, "did you happen to glance out at the highway and see any motorbikes coming or going?"

Fisher closed his eyes again without being prompted this time. When he opened them again, he looked at the sheriff and said, "There was a bike headed off back east --- away from town. I remember it was green. Lime green."#

19

Y ou'd think that the city of Clovis would have been named
for the Clovis people considered by many scientists to be
the first human inhabitants who created an extensive
culture in the New World. The Clovis people are regarded as the
ancestors of most of the indigenous cultures of all the Americas.
Numerous anthropological discoveries of these natives have been
found in the Llano Estacado, the Staked Plains of the Texas
Panhandle and eastern New Mexico --- in fact, just south of the city
close to Portales. But that's not where the name came from. It was
named by the daughter of what was first called "Riley's Switch," a railroad connection point. The station master's daughter had the honor
of naming the place. She picked the name of the first Catholic king of
the Franks --- Clovis --- something she happened to be studying at
the time. The Franks were the first of the known Germanic tribes that
made their home between the Lower and Middle Rhine river valleys
around the third century A.D.

The real claim to fame for Clovis came in the 1950's when a local
musician named Norman Petty set up a recording studio in town and
recorded there with his wife, Vi, and guitarist Jack Vaughn. They
called themselves the Norman Petty Trio and topped the Billboard

charts of the day with their version of the 1930's jazz standard, "Mood Indigo." They had a couple of minor hits but recording "Peggy Sue" for Buddy Holly made their name. Over the years they were one of the studios used by Roy Orbison and Waylon Jennings. To many people that's what Clovis, N.M. is known for.

All of this was more than Tagg Truett knew about his adopted home. He was a man who lived in a small world --- the cowboy titty bar, Billy The Kid's, and his apartment. He liked to think of himself as he was in high school and during his single hitch in the Air Force --- a guy who could bed almost any woman he wanted.

The truth was less flattering. In a part of the country were most people showed their interaction with the outdoors and the sun on their skin, Tagg, living his life in the neon lights of the bar, was pale to the point of being pasty.

When a young woman with great legs and a nice shape over all came in, he figured she was looking for a job as a stripper. She sat down at the bar and let her short denim skirt ride up --- so as she sat sideways, there was an eye catching sight on display.

"The manager's office is back that way," Tagg said with a gesture of his head.

"Why would I be interested in that?" she asked in a husky, smoky voice.

"A job?"

"Got one. Steady pay, benefits, everything Uncle Sam has to offer."

"Air Force?"

"I don't fly'em unless I have to --- but sometimes it comes with the job."

"So what are you doing here?"

"Pour me two fingers of Jim and I'll tell you."

Tagg did as she asked and slid her a tumbler of amber Kentucky liquid which she held up to the light before taking a sip.

"I did my part," he said. "So you're here why?"

"I came for the same reason most of your customers come --- the booze and the view." She held up her glass and toasted Bambi who

was working her way through her set to the half dozen early afternoon regulars. She was twisting around the brass pole on the runway
in the middle of the u-shaped bar where Tagg worked.

"Is that right?" Tagg found himself suddenly interested. "A switch
hitter are you?" He gave her one of his best grins.

"I've discovered that pleasure is where ever you find it." Her eyes
went from the b-cupped dancer to Tagg's smile. "This world is full of
cultures and some are a little more open than others." She downed
the remains of her drink.

"You'll find us wide open," Tagg said refilling her glass. "Especially me."

"Is that so?" she said accepting the drink. "And who exactly are
you?"

"Tagg Truett. Bartender and lady pleasurer all around."

"Talk is very cheap, Mr. Truett."

"Test drives are available upon request."

"Hold up there, dimples. I might be easy --- but one thing I'm not
is fast. I like to take my time --- know that of which I am partaking
before I do partake."

"How about offering a fellow a name?"

"Chaplin. Charlie Chaplin --- with an 'ie'."

"Pleased to meet you Charlie Chaplin --- and glad to see you don't
have a mustache or cane."

"A film aficionado."

"Not so much --- but I do have cable and have seen about every
movie ever made, thanks to TLC being on 24/7. What's your MOS?"

"Three Alpha Oscar double X-ray." This was one Tagg didn't
know and his face registered the fact. "Admin specialist," Charlie said.
"You put in some time or just know the jargon from being around an
air base?"

"One hitch. Double Tango three-seven-zero."

"Internal combustion mechanic."

"Aviation. Bored the hell out of me."

"The benefits of this job are certainly clear." She glanced up at
Bambi again shaking everything she had.

"Her name is Bambi."

"Of course it is," Charlie said without taking her eyes off the performer.

"She's married --- to a biker --- named, Wolf Dice."

"Wolf. I like guys with bikes. Does he share?"

"His bike --- or his wife."

"I could work with either one," she said.

"I've never asked." Tagg wasn't sure where to go with this. "I have a bike," he said.

She then turned back to him.

"And I share," he said.

"Slow down there, dimples. Nobody's asking --- yet." She smiled. "Tell me, where do you live --- if it's with your parents --- we're done."

"I have an apartment --- and a roommate. He's out of town --- for weeks at a time."

"The sharing thing would be better if he was a she --- but things are starting to look up."#

20

L ottie picked up Maude and they went together to the funeral home. They found Beatrice Zollman, the director of the business at her desk.

In high school during her Goth period, Beatrice had been border-line anorexic. Now, approaching thirty, she was at a healthy weight but not suffering any early spread. Naturally small busted, she looked a little androgynous in a suit and tie, but her lipstick and stylish but tasteful black hair said female loudly and clearly.

She and Lottie knew each other from school, but they never hung out together. In fact, Beatrice was primarily a loner until college when she found the man she married, Emanuel (Evan) Alonso. She kept her family name because she had inherited the business when her father died suddenly during her senior year, and she began running it just days out of college.

"Is this a good time?" Lottie asked.

"Perfect," Beatrice said as she closed her paper work and stood offering the two women chairs. "Mother Dickle, Lottie. How are you all holding up?"

"Fine," Lottie said.

"These have been strange days for us."

"I can only imagine," Beatrice said taking her seat again. "That piece Roman Southworth wrote in the Tribune about Jarvis was amazing."

The Muleshoe Tribune was the daily newspaper, and fifty-seven year old Roman was the editor. How he kept the doors open and got it out each week was a wonder to everyone --- but it was a single authoritative source of local news for the town. He had talked to Spencer Lydecker and had gotten the whole story on Jarvis. It was a story nobody knew and was quite a revelation.

"Jarvis brought on himself the life he ended up with here for the past fifteen --- twenty years," Maude said. "If he had only been able to talk about it ...." There was nothing else to say.

"Well, it made more than a few of us ashamed of the way we'd thought about him --- and treated him, I can tell you that."

"Even if we'd known," Lottie said, "without his willingness to change --- to talk to someone --- I don't know how anything would have been different."

"True," Beatrice said. "But I do know that we look at some of the other boys who have been to war and come back changed a lot differently now."

"Then something good did come out of it," Maude said.

"We've come to settle up," Lottie said pulling out the military life insurance policy from her purse. "What do we owe?"

Beatrice made a show of opening a file cabinet and pulling out a folder which she quickly read.

"Exactly --- nothing." She closed the folder.

"I know the pine box was cheap," Maude said, "but nothing is free."

"I didn't say it was free. I said you don't owe anything."

"How come?" Lottie asked.

"It's been taken care of," Beatrice said.

"By whom?"

"People who don't wish to be identified. As a matter of fact, there's more been paid on this account than was owed."

"Somebody just came in and said, 'Put it on my tab?'" Maude asked.

"Not just somebody --- several somebodies."

Lottie and Maude exchanged looks.

"People who felt guilty about the way they had treated my son?"

"They didn't say that. They didn't say much of anything. There were a couple of envelopes with some cash stuck in under the door at night. Some had just a few dollars --- some a lot more. And there were a few checks --- all anonymous."

"I will be damned," Maude said. "And that's not the first time I've said that."

"Thank you, Beatrice," Lottie said standing and offering her hand to this woman she didn't feel she really knew.

"I don't ever say 'It was a pleasure,' because these things never are --- but I was pleased to be able to do what little we could do."

Lottie tried to force a smile to keep from tearing up. She turned toward the door.

"Wait a minute," Maude said. "Give me that insurance policy."

Lottie handed her grandmother the envelope. Maude gave it to Beatrice.

"I've already told you ---."

"This insurance policy was paid for --- and damn sure earned. Use it to cover whatever expenses there are."

Beatrice looked at the document.

"It's worth more than the services provided."

"You charge full fare for Jarvis. If there's anything left over, put it with the money you got from other folks --- and start an account. I'm sure there are always people who need your services but don't have a dime to spare. Take care of them with that --- in Jarvis' name. When that account runs down, you get hold of me or Lottie. You hear?"

It was Beatrice who had to swallow the tears in her throat as Lottie and Maude left. She fell back into her chair stunned.

In the car driving back out to Maude's ranch Lottie said, "Thanks, Nana. That was wonderful."

"Not so much. Notice I didn't give any of my money away. It's you who'll have to cough up something in the future."

"I think I'll be able to manage that. The financial advisor Mr. Creighton sent me to thinks we can make all of Daddy's money grow --- and I won't have to touch the principal."

"You told anybody about that money?"

"No. Didn't figure it was anybody's business."

"Smart, girl. Very smart."

"There is one thing I've been wondering about? How well do you and Caroline get along --- I mean when you're together for more than a few hours?"

"Honey, Caroline is the sister I never had."

"Neither one of you are getting any younger."

"You ready to ship us off to Shady Pines somewhere together?"

"I was thinking more of having her move in with you."

"Me?"

"We could get the house fixed up so all the doors are wide enough for her wheelchair and walker --- a ramp in the front and back --- one of those staircase-riding seats on the stairs. Fix up the down stairs bath so it would easy for her. She could teach you the Internet and you could ---."

"What? What can I do for her?"

"The little things she has trouble with. Keep each other company. Together you two would be one bitchin' ol' lady."

Maude thought about the idea for a few moments.

"We sure would. Maybe even two bitchin' ol' ladies --- on wheels."

#

21

"We have permission to confiscate the bike."

Martin Ybarra, Curry County, New Mexico, Sheriff was speaking into his desk phone to his colleague Asa Hunt, Bailey County, Texas, Sheriff.

"Way to go, Martin. How'd you swing that?"

"We located Coy Vanderveer, Tagg Truett's apartment roommate. He's near Boston and is going on up to Maine before he heads back.

"Damn, when they call them 'long haul truckers' they're not kidding. Did he balk at the idea at all?"

"Not in the least. He's going to e-mail us a digitally signed permission once he finishes his breakfast and cranks up his truck."

"He's got e-mail in his truck?"

"Have you seen the insides of these semi-tractors these days? They look like a Space X capsule. The only reason he's got a fax is because his company isn't totally digital, yet. Evidently they've been sold and bought a few times in the last couple of years --- and they're not all on the same page with software and tracking. So, it's not a problem."

"What a stroke of luck. And I'm saying this as somebody who still relies on my fax machine."

"Oh, we do, too," Sheriff Ybarra chuckled. "So you want to come over for a sit down with Truett?"

"Love to. My wife needs me to get something for one of the grand-kids at Walmart, so I was coming over unofficially anyway."

"Then make if official. I'll send a deputy out and politely ask Tagg to come down to the office --- let's say right after lunch."

"Your shop?"

"No, on second thought, let's go to his bar."

"Billy The Kid's."

"Look at it this way --- if they ever make a movie of this, they'll want a scene with cops in a strip bar. It's almost obligatory."

"Life doesn't usually emulate art --- if you can call it art. One thirty?"

"See you here, Sheriff."

"Looking forward to it, Sheriff."

LOTTIE RECORDED two commercials to finish up her shift at the radio station. Her next appointment was in Jarvis' workshop.

Waiting for her was a stooped shouldered, soft academic with a middle-age spread. Lottie got out of her truck and opened one of the steel accordion doors. The man approached and offered her a business card which read: Malcom Kiniston, Ph.D. Professor/Curator, Panhandle–Plains Historical Museum, West Texas A&M, Canyon, TX.

"Professor Kiniston," Lottie said reading the card. "I recognize your name from somewhere but I'm having trouble placing it."

"I would expect you have seen or heard of one of my books."

"Books?"

"I'm a Texas historian. West Texas is my specialty. Do the titles, Comanche Canyon, Red River Indian War, or XIT, The Ranch That Made The Panhandle mean anything to you?"

"The first one. I read it in college."

"It's been around a while."

"Look around," Lottie said as she flipped on the lights. "Help yourself." She used the pulley-chains to hoist the second bay door on opposite side of the shop for even more light.

There was still the tape outline of where Jarvis' body had been on the floor. The blood which had oozed from his head had been cleaned up.

She looked around the shop feeling very much out of place there as she always had.

After a good twenty minutes or so, Kiniston turned to Lottie who was leaning against one wall in the shade.

"Do you know what you have here?"

"Farrier tools."

"A couple are almost two-hundred years old. Several aren't made any more and haven't been for years."

"So you are interested in some of them?"

"Some? All of them. With a few exceptions this would be what a farrier's shop would look like before Texas won its independence in 1836."

The professor pulled out his cell phone and activated the camera. He took a dozen pictures from almost every imaginable angle.

"We could set up a display based on what's here that would be unique."

"I guess that's why Daddy thought your museum would be the place for this stuff."

"Stuff. You don't grasp what I'm saying, Ms. Truett. This is a real working blacksmith shop set back into the past. Your father must have been a man of principals and taste to have collected all this."

"I wish I could say one way or the other," Lottie said. "I didn't know my father very well."

"I'm sorry to hear that."

"So am I," she said, "--- now."

"To be a farrier who specialized in mules --- and obviously knew his tools --- your father was a remarkable man."

"I am beginning to appreciate that."

"What do you know about mules?"

"They're a cross between a horse and a donkey."

The professor waited a moment before he spoke.

"That's about most people's limited understanding. Without giving you the whole course, let me enlighten you just a little."

"Please," Lottie said.

"Nobody knows where the first mules originated. Wild donkeys and horses cross bred and remains have been found in parts of what is today Turkey. Remember the Hittites from the Bible? Well, they considered a mule to be three times the value of a horse.

"A mule is the product of a male donkey, a jack, and a female horse. A horse has 64 chromosomes and a donkey has 62. A mule has 63.

"If you bred a male horse with a female donkey you get a hinny --- not as big or as strong as a mule.

"A female mule, a molly, isn't sterile but a male is.

"A mule is stronger than a horse, can run or walk longer than a horse. In a distance race a mule will always out last a horse. It has harder hooves than horses, is easier to train --- and although a mule has a reputation of being stubborn, the truth is a mule is smarter than a horse. A horse will work itself to death --- a mule won't. He or she will stop and work no more when it has had as much as it can take.

"The tools and the set-up your father had here show me he was a man who knew all this and more. He appreciated mules and went to a great deal of trouble to make sure he was able to tend to them the right way."

"My father was a man who suffered from PTSD --- and nobody knew it. He closed everyone close to him out of his life. I believe now he thought he was keeping his pain away from us. I am very glad you can see the value of what he did and that you can put his tools to a good use."

"They will be a gift to Texas and to history."#

22

T he two sheriffs parked side by side and went into Billy The Kid's stripper bar together. It took a moment for their vision to adjust. Then the two lawmen made their way through the dark and took seats at the bar behind Tagg Truett who was focused on the dancer performing behind him.

She was better endowed than real women and she was using her augmented assets to her best advantage, hanging upside down on the first brass poll up near the stage entrance. If a man could draw his eyes to her face, the platinum blonde and crows feet showed her true years in this business and the mandatory hard life that went along with it. Heavy make-up couldn't hide that she only had a few years left in this career.

"Tagg Truett?" Sheriff Ybarra said after a full minute when the bartender kept his eyes glued to the performer.

The thirty-six year old spun and tried to force a smile which instantly faded when the pair of sheriffs registered in his mind.

"Tagg," Sheriff Hunt said.

"This isn't two-for-one day. But we do offer special pricing to those who protect and serve."

"All we want is a little conversation," the younger sheriff said.

"If you'd like, Tagg," Asa said, "we can move over to a table and we can sit with our backs to the stage so you don't miss anything."

"I know everything Crystal's got --- intimately."

"She still seem to have your full attention."

"Planning ahead. What do you two want to know?"

"You know Jarvis Dickle was murdered?"

"Oh, good news travels fast. I heard about it the day it happened."

Sheriff Ybarra sat back and let Asa take the lead.

"Where were you that morning? Say between 6 and 8?"

"You ran out of people who hated Jarvis in Texas so you decided to cross the state line --- see if you can't pin it on somebody over here?"

"That's not an answer, Tagg."

"What day was that --- a Monday?"

"Tuesday."

"If it was Tuesday, it was my day off. But like the rest of my week, I don't get up til' about two in the afternoon."

"Anybody can vouch for that? Like Crystal there?"

"I'm sure if I ask her just right, she'd say we were together."

"And what if we ask her?"

"Without the proper context, she might not remember. See Crystal doesn't remember a lot of things exactly right. Truth is, she wasn't there. I was by myself --- asleep. That's why I have aluminum foil on my windows and a 'Day Sleeper' sign on my front door."

"When was the last time you were in Muleshoe?"

"Over a year ago. Sheriff, I ain't lost nothing in that town. Since Lottie and I busted up, I've sort of lost all interest in Texas."

"But you've been divorced more than four years. You've pass through at least during that time."

"Oh, I didn't stop in town. I had business in Lubbock --- checking out some possible talent for the boss. I only slowed down for the stop lights."

"And Jarvis? When was the last time you saw him?"

"The night he shot me."

"Not since then?"

"I had no reason to see that son of a bitch."

"Why didn't you press charges? Assault with a deadly weapon would have put ol' Jarvis in the pen."

"Because I wanted to get out your town and stay out. Check it out. I signed our divorce papers over here. I told Lottie I wasn't comin' back just for that."

Crystal finished her number and looked disappointed that Tagg was otherwise engaged as she left the stage. He did turn and give her one of his smiles before she disappeared behind the stage curtains.

Turning back to the lawmen Tagg ran his tongue around his teeth.

"There are two sheriffs' cars parked out front aren't there?"

"This is official business," Sheriff Martin Ybarra said. He turned to Asa, "Sheriff Hunt, did I leave my flasher on by mistake?"

"Shit," Tagg threw the bar towel over his shoulder in a wad on the bar. "Okay, what's it going to take to get you two out of here?"

"A few answers," Sheriff Ybarra said.

"Straight answers," Asa Hunt clarified.

"I didn't kill Jarvis Dickle. I'd like to thank whoever did, but it wasn't me. I wasn't there. I was asleep --- in my bed --- in my apartment."

"Alone?" Asa asked.

"Totally and absolutely alone!"

"I thought you were a real lady's man, Tagg?"

Tagg bit his lip for a moment before he spoke.

"Not like I used to be. Not since I had a chunk of my ass blown off. I still walk with a limp."

"And you've never tried telling people it was a war wound?"

"Go to hell!"

"I just thought you would have worked every angle you could, Tagg. You used to. At least that's what Lottie says."

"That bitch?"

"What did she ever do to you? As I understand it she never once cheated on you. Can you say the same thing?"

Tagg had no answer for that question. He tightened his jaw and took a deep breath.

"You own a bike, Tagg."

"Bicycle?"

"No, motorbike."

"No. I have a vet."

"Corvette? Nice."

"It ain't new, but I take care of it. It'll do."

"Not like your wife?"

"I've got nothing more to say about Lottie."

"Got any friends that have a motorbike?"

"Some of the guys of some of the girls that work here have Harleys. I don't count any of them as friends."

"Anyone else?"

"Not that I know of. It's not something I'm interested in."

There was silence between the three for a few moments. Only the throbbing of the music being blasted out of the sound system was heard and another performer took the stage.

"Well, we should let you get back to business."

"Thanks to you I don't have any business."

The sheriffs left together.

"What do you think?" the Curry County Sheriff asked when they were outside.

"I think we shook him up a little. Did you notice he didn't even glance at the new girl when she came out --- and she was a looker? And one thing I do know about Tagg is that he pays attention to good looking women."#

23

S aturday night Dallas's band, The Staked Planes, played at a dance in the Muleshoe Ballroom. The band's emblem, a crop duster with a bloody wooden stake through its cockpit and musical notes, boots and cowboy hats spewing out of its wing nozzles, was on Judd's drum as the five piece group cranked out country music to the packed hall. The Muleshoe Ballroom had begun life as a department store, but it had been years since any legitimate retail business had been conducted there.

Even now, aside for the price of admission nothing was for sale inside the ballroom. Bailey County was a dry county so it was either BYOB or deal with the sales of beers and Mary Jane under the table. The off duty city patrolman who served as security was busy looking the other way all night.

Like most of downtown, time, the West Texas agriculture econ-omy, and the declining population had left the down town buildings standing but mostly empty. The Wallace movie theatre across the street was boarded up and had been for years.

Judd Tillman was Dallas's airplane mechanic and one third partner during the week. Come the weekend he turned into the drummer for The Staked Planes. The curly mop of red hair bounced and flew as one of Dallas' former high school linemen worked the trap set and cymbals with passion and a giant grin.

The Staked Planes had started life as a punk rock garage band working out of an empty hanger at Dallas' father's crop dusting business. Over the years as members came and went, it became clear that a West Texas band that didn't play country wasn't going to get either gigs or income. The name of the band hadn't changed but Dallas had picked up the banjo and learned to play it as well at rhythm guitar which he already knew. He and Juan Cano shared vocals while Juan played base guitar.

They kept trading lead guitar players --- the current one was Pat Rangle, great fingers and the most fun to work with of the last three. He was short except for his long fingers and had a poker face no matter how simple or complicated the riff was he was working through. Pat's day job was auto parts.

What had committed the band to country music was the addition of Scotty McGuire, Mexican chef by day but a fiddle player who could also play Dobro guitar, mandolin and even switch off with Pat on lead guitar by night.

As the band worked through their first set and the beer flowed, Lottie slipped in. She didn't often show up to Dallas' engagements because it wasn't much fun sitting and watching. She would dance when asked, but country music was her world half of every day --- so she didn't mind a few hours away on the weekends when Dallas' band usually played out of town. This occasion was a swap-off with another band who covered for The Staked Planes in Amarillo during the weekend following Jarvis' murder.

Dallas spotted Lottie as soon as she began edging her way towards one of the tables in the back. After the band's current number, Dallas turned back to the guys and they changed the upcoming song. As the music began, Lottie recognized the tune.

What she didn't expect was Dallas stepping up to the mic while the band vamped behind him.

"We have a personality in the house!" he announced. "Our own Lottie Truett from Muleshoe radio!"

He motioned toward her and the crowd responded with applause. Everybody in town knew Lottie on sight and she always felt she was about as much a personality as the postman. Still she stood and waved to the crowd.

"I want to announce tonight that Lottie and I are engaged," Dallas said when the clapping died down. The crowd was pumped back up and there were whistles and yells added.

"I had to say that before Inez finds out at the Coffee Mug."

Everyone laughed.

"One thing Inez and nobody else but Lottie and I know is that we signed a prenup two days ago."

This surprised Lottie because she hadn't even told Maude. This was a secret she was keeping in her heart --- very much a private thing.

The crowd like this prenup idea and particularly the women clapped and whistled.

"Under the terms of our deal," Dallas went on putting his banjo down on the instrument stand beside himself on the stage, "if this marriage doesn't work out, Lottie gets both my banjo and the band. So you know I'm going to work my *ass* off to make sure it works."

This produced laughter and more applause.

"You're all invited --- when we set the date --- which we haven't --- yet --- but once we do, I expect to be spending the next sixty years doing what Billy Talmadge --- the nephew of Earnest Tubb --- wrote about. Juan's going to do the vocal on this one --- and I'm going to start my Waltz Across Texas with Lottie in my arms.

The band picked up as Dallas came down and met Lottie in the middle of the dance floor. He whirled her around and they swept across the area as everyone in the place joined in.

As they danced, Lottie said in Dallas' ear, "I thought you were going to...."

He cut her off, "That's nobody's business but ours. I think you're wise not to go out and spend any of it for a year."

"Well ---," she started.

"What did you do?" he laughed.

"I think I've talked Caroline into moving in with Nana. That's going to require a few adjustments to Nana's place."

"I don't consider that spending. If anything, it's an investment."

"I knew you'd understand," she said as she hugged him.

"Besides," Dallas smiled, "I think I just saved us a bundle on invitations."

Lottie couldn't help but laugh, and she felt propelled into the stars as they danced.#

24

The District Attorney for Bailey County also served as the prosecutor for Parmer County directly north on the Texas/New Mexico border. Alfonzo (call me 'Al') Greason, officially the D.A. for the 287th Judicial District, was freckled with green eyes. He stood 6 foot 7 inches and had been a Heisman Trophy candidate. His gridiron career ended when his left ankle was shattered in a tackle during the Cotton Bowl game against North Carolina. Not a handsome man, Al Greason had a Roman nose, and even at 42, sagging jowls and plenty of extra weight.

Sheriff Asa Hunt had given the files and the assignment to get an arrest warrant from Greason to his deputy, Polly Clover. She was one day going to be a sheriff or a chief of police and this was an experience she needed. Greason was always combative when presented with a possible felony case and had to be convinced in his heart of the guilt of the person to be accused.

The folder was two and a half inches thick that Deputy Clover handed to the D.A.

"Have a seat, Deputy," Greason said and he accepted the folder and opened it on his desk. "The Jarvis Dickle murder, huh? What took so long?"

"It wasn't a domestic dispute or either an alcohol or drug related killing. This one was planned and the suspect intended to get away with it."

"Don't they all?"

"No, sir. Often they turn themselves in the next day or two and confess what they've done. Murder is usually a crime of passion and once the passion cools --- humans who are not psycho or sociopaths tend to harbor deep regret."

"Is that was Asa tells you?"

"It's what I've seen for myself."

"Then we're on the same page, Deputy."

Greason spent the next several minutes reading through the evidence, the interview statements, and looking at the pictures of both the crime scene and of the evidence.

When he eventually looked up at Deputy Clover, the D.A. asked, "Did you ever know Jarvis Dickle?"

"No, sir. He was pointed out to me a few times so I knew what he looked like --- but our paths never really crossed."

"Putting aside what the long story in The Muleshoe Stake said and the fact that he may have served his country well and with honor --- Jarvis Dickle was still a bastard. I don't consider P.T.S.D. as a get-out-of-jail-free card. Do you know how hard it's going to be to find a dozen people in these two counties who aren't, secretly in their hearts, glad he's gone?"

"No, sir. That's not my job."

"Damn right, it's not your job. And now that you've dropped the steaming pile of mule turds on my desk it *is* my problem."

"So you recommend an arrest warrant?"

"One man's already dead and now it's going to be my job to try and kill another one --- and all you care about is a warrant?"

"What I care about, Mr. Greason, is justice. I have a part to play in the process --- and so do you. We in the sheriff's office have done ours. What we do isn't all paperwork and words. We get down in the blood and mud. We don't frame people, plant evidence, or make closing cases our number one priority. Every day when we put on our badges and guns, we pray we won't have to shoot someone and that we'll come home to those we love with a clear conscious and knowing we did something to promote justice. No, we're not charged with trying to take anyone's life unless it's in self-defense. But our job, just like yours, sir, is voluntary. Any time it gets to be too much, we can always walk away and hope somebody else will pick up the duty."

Greason sat back and studied the uniformed young woman across from him.

He nodded his head slowly as he said, "I hope you never lose your passion for what you do, Deputy. I went to law school to do this job because I believe in justice, too, --- but I don't think I could do your job. I'll get you your warrant within an hour."

Polly Clover, caught a little off guard by the D.A.'s comment, stood and said, "Thank you, sir."

AN ARREST WARRANT isn't an impressive document. It's a boiler plate legal form with a county's logo at the top, several lines to print and blank spaces for the arrestee, the bond amount, and a signatory block for the issuing judge.

Tagg Truett was arrested trying to load his car in front of his apartment in Clovis. The New Mexico, Curry County Sheriff's Office conducted the arrest. He was Mirandized as he was handcuffed. He was booked into the sheriff's jail.

The next order of business was extradition. When Judd was taken before a judge, he was given the opportunity to request an extradition hearing, but his assigned Public Defender told him than if he did, he was opening himself up to a charge of fleeing the jurisdiction where the crime, the murder of Jarvis Dickle, was committed. Regardless of anything else this could add an additional five to ten years prison time. As per usual, the defendant waved the extradition hearing and was handed over to Texas, Bailey County deputies for transport to Muleshoe.

The next morning he was officially arraigned on the charge of capital murder, and he was assigned a Texas public defender because he said he did not have the money to pay a lawyer. His lawyer stood by Judd's side as the formal process was conducted. Once back in the Bailey County Jail, Judd had his first long meeting with his attorney.#

25

Roberta Osburn was the local liberal in Muleshoe. Any controversy would find her with printed signs and a bull horn in front of the county court house, city hall on 1st Street, or whatever government agency involved or implicated in the matter, well before all the facts were clear. She was also the number one choice of Judge Lonie Fitzmore before he recused himself from the case. Like everyone else in town, he had his run ins with Jarvis and didn't feel it was proper for him to be the judge on the bench for the case.

Tagg's first exposure to his public defender was in a bleak interrogation room with a thick glass mirror on one side of the pink painted room and a mounted camera up in one corner.

Roberta was brusk and after introducing herself, the full figured woman who was pushing the envelope toward obese put her twisted head of grey and white hair down and searched through the file before her. She was a dark skinned Hispanic with a lazy eye making her sometimes appear cross-eyed as she peered through thick lens.

Without looking up she said, "Tagg Truett, I am your lawyer. You can lie to your girlfriend, your mistress, to your boss, to your brother, to your priest --- but don't lie to me. Be brutally honest with me. I'm the only one who is completely on your side in this. Whatever you say to me is just between us --- and I won't utter a syllable of it without your permission."

She looked up and studied his face before she said, "I'm only going to ask you this one time --- but everything will depend on a flat out honest answer. Lie to me now, and you've screwed yourself for all time to come. Do you understand?"

Tagg nodded slowly. The gravity of what was happening had all sunk in on him.

"Did you kill Jarvis Dickle?"

Tagg just as slowly shook his head as he said, "No, I did not. I'm glad the son-of-a-bitch is dead --- but it wasn't me that had the pleasure."

Roberta smiled or at least moved her cheeks in what would pass for a smile.

"I knew Jarvis --- and I understand. In some ways I'm sorry I didn't have the pleasure, myself."

Tagg's face fell.

"You believe me?"

"Yes, son, I do. And I'll do everything I can to help prove that fact."

Tagg opened his mouth and breathed as he dropped back in his chair.

"Nobody else believes me."

"You've been dealing with cops. It's their job not to. They try to keep you away from anybody who does believe you."

"I don't know who that'd be."

"Me, for one. And I'm shrewd, astute, and as cunning as I am intense. I don't take shit from anyone --- and people only make the mistake of giving me crap just once --- never again. So, relax and let's get started. Right now, it's you and me against the world --- but, son, I'm damn good at what I do. Don't B.S. me and we'll do all right."

"You mean," Tagg said sitting forward, "you think you can get me off?"

"Maybe not the first time --- but we have a long road ahead of us here. Judge Fitzmore recused himself from the case because he knew

Jarvis and didn't like him any better than you or anybody else did. Let's see who pops up as the visiting judge. Anybody is better than Hardass Fitzmore.

"And let's be realistic, if we can't get a change of venue and they do hold the trial here, that can be a good thing for us. Even if we lose. It makes it a lot easier to get a retrial --- with a different judge and a more favorable jury."

She turned back to all the paperwork saying, "So put on your deep waders, and your work gloves --- and hang the hell on. This is going to be a muddy and tough road --- but we're in this together."

Tagg ran all this through his head before he said, "Thank you, Ms. Osburn."

"I can't say the pleasure is mine, son, because this isn't going to be fun for either of us."

Judge Seward Kulpepper from Lubbock was assigned the case. The almost skeletal thin jurist with no hair, not even eyebrows, was known to be a judicial activist. He was known to run a strict court-room under very authoritarian rules. As unlikely as his choice seemed, Roberta Osburn told Tagg that both she and the judge had met a couple of times over the years at liberal political functions. She didn't expect him to cut her much slack, but she might be able to play the man a little if the occasion demanded.

For Tagg, the long days sitting in his pink painted cell were lonely and depressing. The idea of doing serious time in a penitentiary frightened him. Although he seemed to have some automatic respect from some of the other few inmates that came and went because of the seriousness of his crime, this was not a world Tagg thought he could ever thrive in.

He had a couple of visits from girls who worked in the Clovis bar and even one from the manager --- but it was evident that they all believed him to be guilty of the crime. The only thing in his future was the trial and strangely enough, he began anticipating it.

Outside the wall of the jail life was going on. One of the guards gladly shared his story of deer hunting one weekend with Dallas in a voice intended for Tagg to hear.

"Got a ten point buck. Dallas was all pissed --- he didn't get to fire a shot. Said he had a twelve pointer all lined up when my shot spooked him. He was so pissed I thought we were going to have to strap him across the hood to get him home."

"Oh, the one that got away," another guard laughed.

The first guard mentioned that Dallas and Lottie were going to celebrate the end of the trial by getting married.

The conversation had the desired effect. Tagg told Roberta this was the most miserable day of his life. He could have been happy with Lottie --- but he couldn't behave himself.

Roberta got his mind off his troubles by bringing in some clothes for Tagg to try on. He didn't own a suit or tie himself, but she found one in a second hand store which fit. She promised to have the suit cleaned an pressed before he wore it to court.#

26

M uleshoe is a place that's used to sorting steers from beers. But after two days of trying Judge Seward Kulpepper decided they weren't going to find a jury without a dozen people who hadn't already made up their mind about Jarvis Dickle. He told public defender Roberta Osburn he would be happy to entertain a motion for change of venue. She so moved and not only did Judge Kulpepper entertain the idea, he threw it a damn fandango. He moved the trial up to Amarillo, lock, stock, witnesses and defendant.

What this meant was that if you were involved in the proceedings, you could either rent a hotel room at Bailey County's expense or enjoy a ninety mile drive to and from the Potter County Court House. It was a chance to enjoy all the open space and very few trees between the two locations. Plus there was the joy of having Hereford, "Beef Capital of the World" as the high point of your trip. The local *aroma* was money to the locals while everyone else held their noses as they pushed the speed limit going through town. The methane laced odor of the multiple cattle feed yards which was the town's primary source of income and B.S. was the smell of money.

The Potter County Court House, on 501 South Taylor Street, was, like the Sante Fe building, an early 1930 art deco structure. There was a newer County Court House but out of town cases were often given the joy of being held in the older building with its Texas Historic Landmark status. Of course, if you were on trial for your life, as Tagg Truett was, the historical significance of the surroundings held very little appeal.

Alfonzo Greason, the Bailey and Parmer D.A., was still prosecuting. His slight cleft palette, he always believed adequately cloaked by his drooping mustache and van dyke beard of strawberry red, in addition to years of work with specialists, left little trace of the birth defect in his speech or appearance. His wide eyes gave him the overall countenance of a walrus. His bulk added to the picture, but Greason was always perfectly groomed and uniformed in a three piece suit.

When Greason stepped up to give his opening argument, he projected an air of total confidence and self-assuredness which rung in every word he spoke.

"This case is about the senseless murder of a man who was not well liked in our small town," Greason began. "Jarvis Dickle, we have learned since his death, had suffered for years from P.T.S.D. from his heroic time in Iraq and Afghanistan. He was awarded multiple Purple Hearts and even put up for the Congressional Medal of Honor --- but suffering from survivor's guilt, he refused to accept it --- and only took the Silver Star after a direct order from his commander to do so.

"After his times in hell, he came home to a wife who had died of cancer while he was at war, and to a daughter he hardly knew and certainly didn't know how to raise. Even his own mother didn't understand the power of the after effects of her son's time in harm's way. He tried to make himself a life as a mule farrier just outside of town in a shop where he worked alone with the animals he treated so well.

"You will hear Jarvis Dickle described as an S.O.B. --- among other things --- and no one who ever encountered him since returning from battle would argue that assent. Still, he was a man, a law abiding man, a veteran, and the best at what he did of anyone in Texas, New Mexico, Arizona, Colorado, Kansas, or Oklahoma."

Greason raked his gaze over the seven men and five women who made up the jury.

"We will grant that Jarvis Dickle wasn't a nice guy. In fact, he wasn't even close. He didn't try to be and didn't care to be.

"What he didn't deserve, however, was to die by having three nails driven into the top of his head --- stunning him and then taking his life on the floor of his workshop."

The District Attorney paced in front of the jury a moment before he continued.

"But for one man, Jarvis Dickle would be with us today --- still irritating everyone he met but doing a masterful job of taking care of some of God's lowest creatures. The man who took it upon himself to kill Jarvis was his former son-in-law," he gestured to the defense table where Tagg sat with Roberta. "Tagg Truett --- who didn't even live in Muleshoe anymore --- concocted an elaborate plot to feloniously murder Jarvis Dickle and go back to his own miserable, pointless life as if nothing had happened.

"We will prove it to you so that you will not have the least doubt how Jarvis Dickle died --- how the act was committed --- and who the coward was who did the deed. When this trial is over, we will ask you to sentence that man there," again pointing to Tagg, "to death by lethal injection --- a much kinder death than the one he dealt to his former father-in-law."

Alfonzo Greason had timed his speech so he had to cross from the jury box back to the prosecution table where it almost looked as if he was about to beach his substance on his table before he rounded the corner and sat. His words hung in the air.

Judge Kulpepper nodded toward Roberta Osburn , "Defense," he said, "your opening remarks."

Roberta heaved herself out of her chair and crossed right up to the jury. All the members of the panel were thinking the same things: "How could those ankles sustain their burden?" and "This was going to be a heavy weight fight."

"The accused is 'innocent until proven guilty,' ladies and gentle-men. My client, Mr. Tagg Truett sits before you unconvicted --- but also unheard. Don't make the mistake of deciding he is a killer until you hear all the evidence.

"The evidence you will hear, while a good story, is so loosely based on facts that you would not want to have your own life depend on this little or nothing. There are coincidences, circumstances which might *suggest* fact, but circumstances and suggestions do not hard facts make. A man's life is in the balance of Lady Justice --- you --- and all we ask is that you not make up your mind until you've heard everything.

"If you can --- imagine yourself sitting over there accused of a crime you did not commit --- and decide how you would like the twelve people who sit in judgement of you to look up on you. Not guilty because the prosecution says he is --- not guilty until there is before you hard evidence that tells you he committed this crime. You know how you feel right now --- innocent --- but put yourself in that chair --- and treat this man just as you would like to be treated. That will give us true justice."#

27

L ottie, Maude, and Maude's best friend, Caroline Montoya got an extended stay room at a Holiday Inn for the duration of the trial. Lottie had her own room for the nights when Dallas could come up and join her. He flew into Rich Husband Airport in his crop duster and Lottie would meet him there. Dallas never got to the trial because he had to fly back every day except Sunday to work.

D.A. Alfonzo Greason's strategy for the trial was to employ a large rolling white board on which he created a timeline of events. The star three quarters down the line was the place where he detailed the murder.

Before he called his first witness, the D.A. submitted Jarvis' military record into evidence --- reading from the presentations of his awards and showing the Purple Hearts and finally the Silver Star before placing them on the evidence table. He also tried to read part of the piece published in The Muleshoe Stake by editor Roman Southworth about Jarvis once his military record was known. But defense council Roberta Osburn stood and said, "The defense will stipulate to Mr. Dickle's military record and awards as long as the prosecution will admit that most everyone in town would cross the street to keep from having to even speak to the deceased?"

"The man was murdered, your Honor. A few words on his character don't seem too out of place"

"As long as you admit what kind of person Jarvis Dickle was --- war hero or not. Even Adolph Hitler could paint a picture. Nobody misses him now that he's dead. Jarvis Dickle was not the Saint of Muleshoe."

"If the defense is trying to compare the deceased to Adolph Hitler..." the D.A. shot back.

Judge Kulpepper banged his gavel on his desk.

"Enough! Will the prosecution agree that the murdered Mr. Dickle was not a well liked person?"

"Your Honor," Ms. Osburn said, "people don't like skunks --- they didn't have *that* much admiration for Jarvis Dickle."

"I said enough!"

Prosecutor Greason thought for a moment and then said, "We will acknowledge a strong, general dislike of the people of Muleshoe for Mr. Dickle."

"Ms. Osburn, is that sufficient for the defense?"

Knowing she had already made the point herself to the jury, Roberta Osburn nodded her head and wedged herself back in her seat.

The first witness was Fisher Minard, the barrel chested, brown eyed, no ear lobed package delivery driver who discovered Jarvis' body. As he testified, Greason produced crime scene photographs so the jury would get a vivid image of the site. After passing the pictures to the empaneled jurors he affixed each to the whiteboard around the star.

On cross examination Ms. Osburn was able to establish that the driver did not in fact see her client on the lime green motorbike that he only barely remembered.

"The helmented rider you saw could have been anyone from Darth Vader to Daisy Duck --- isn't that correct, Mr. Minard? He --- or she --- could have been black, Asian, even Martian for all you know?"

"I guess," the driver said.

"Guess? Mr. Minard, a man's life is at stake here. Can you or can you not tell us if it was Tagg Truett you saw on that motorbike?"

"I can't."

"No more questions for this witness."

"Recross, your Honor" Greason said without moving from his chair.

"Mr. Greason," the Judge said.

"Mr. Minard, can you tell us if it could possibly have been Mr. Truett?"

"Objection!" Roberta Osburn hadn't even made it back to her chair when she turned on the D.A. "The witness has already stated he could not say who the rider was. The prosecution is asking for speculation from the witness not facts. If we're going to start guessing who that rider might have been, I would like to add the names of Justin Bieber, Jimmy Fallon, and Elvis Presley to the possibilities."

"Objection sustained," the judge pronounced. "The witness may step down."

Maude whispered to Caroline and Lottie, "I've never liked Roberta Osburn but if they ever arrest me, call her to be my lawyer."

The next witness was Hazen Snead, the Clovis, N.M. ranch owner who had brought two mules into Jarvis earlier the same morning the mule farrier was killed. The D.A. managed to make a few points toward rehabilitating Jarvis' character with Hazen's story about why he though so highly of the dead man's work with mules. But other than establishing that he had an encounter with someone on a green motorbike he had little to add to the time line.

Again the defense was able to establish that the witness never saw the bike again --- not around Jarvis' workshop nor in town. Greason tried to point out that the bike could have been parked on the far side of the closed workshop while Hazen put his animals in the attached corral. Roberta Osburn pointed out that the bike could have also gone on through town. Although the bike both witnesses described was green, lime green, there was no way to prove it was the same bike driven by the same person.

The afternoon was taken up with the testimony of the Bailey county coroner, 40's, frumpy and disheveled Dr. Betsy Sue Darvel. She detailed her autopsy and her expert opinion that Jarvis was attacked from behind. She pointed out the damage the first nail had done and how she believed it was the loss of blood and the damage of the second two nails that were responsible for his death.

Lottie phoned the radio station as soon as court was adjourned for the day. She was the on-the-scene reporter for the station. But because of her involvement, Webb never used any of her actual reports which he recorded. Lottie managed to stick to the facts of each day's events in her phone calls and thus gave the station a twice a day story of the on going trial.

After dropping off Maude and Caroline at the motel, she met Dallas at the airport and then drove back into town where the four found a different restaurant to eat in each night. Nobody said it, but thanks to Jarvis, these were some of the best nights out the three women had enjoyed in years.#

28

The first witness the next day was an attractive Air Force officer in her dress uniform. She was introduced as Major Charlie Chaplin of the Air Police as she was sworn in.

Tagg grabbed his attorney's arm and quietly told her, "I thought she was a bi-slut who was looking to get laid."

"You know her?" Roberta Osburn asked.

"She came in the bar once."

"You talked to her?"

"Yeah. I thought she was a nice piece of ass on the make."

"What did you tell her?"

"Nothing," Tagg said not understanding what was going on.

Major Chaplin took the witness chair as Alfonzo Greason informed the court that the young woman was appearing on behalf of Curry County Sheriff's Office --- where she had been used as a confidential informant.

"The information Major Chaplin will present is contained on this CD," the prosecutor said entering the recording in evidence.

"Point of order, your Honor," the Defense Attorney said.

"Ms. Osburn?" the judge asked.

"This witness is appearing here as a C.I. for another jurisdiction --- another state?"

"Sheriff Martin Ybarra and his office were cooperating and assisting in this investigation," the D.A. responded.

"And how does an Air Force officer become a C.I.?"

"Cannon Air Force Base and Curry County have been coordinating their law enforcement activities for years."

When Roberta Osburn appeared to have no more questions, Judge Kulpepper motioned towards the D.A. "Continue."

The essence of Major Chaplin's testimony was to establish that Tagg claimed to have a motorbike. Once that was on the record, the D.A. turned the witness over to the defense.

"All this conversation was recorded?" she asked.

"I was wearing a wire," the Major said.

"Oh, I'm sure. And we're not talking about just in your bra either are we?" Without waiting for a response the defense attorney want on, "And you had no intention of going to bed with my client, either did you?"

The major held up her left hand and displayed a wedding ring.

"My husband and I have this monogamy thing going."

Alfonzo Greason climbed out of his chair as he said, "Neither New Mexico or Texas have duel party recording consent, your Honor. Under U.S.C. 2511(2)(d)," he picked up two Xeroxed sheets of paper off of his table handing one to the defense and the other to the judge, "the recording is legal."

"Okay," Roberta said, "but what's the point?"

"My next two witness, New Mexico Curry County Sheriff Martin Ybarra and Texas Bailey County Sheriff Asa Hunt will testify that the defendant claimed to them that he did *not*, in fact, have a motorbike --- nor did he have any friends who did."

"Your Honor, need I cross exam this witness to prove she never identified herself as a legal authority?"

"The prosecution will so stipulate," Alfonzo said.

"Then let's not waste the courts time proving that a guy who works in a strip club will tell an attractive woman whatever she wants to hear if it gets him where he wants her --- namely, in bed."

"Major Chaplin never left the bar with the defendant, your Honor. Nor did she ever promise to."

"There are several steps to the seduction dance which I doubt I need to explain to either your Honor or to the Prosecution. So he told her he had a bike because that's what she wanted to hear. He told the authorities the truth. He didn't. If this is about trying to make my client out to be a liar ...."

"It is," Greason admitted, "and we'll prove it."

"Over a motorbike he didn't own?"

"Over a motorbike he says none of his friends owns either."

"For the sake of brevity, your Honor, because this is like pulling teeth with a hammer, let's say the defense agrees that my client told one story to this witness but told the truth to the law?"

"Then we can skip over Sheriff Hunt for the moment, dismiss Sheriff Ybarra and move on to our next prosecution witness," the D.A. said.

"Please, God," Alberta said heading back to her chair with her copy of the Xerox legal form in her hand.

"You are dismissed," Judge Kulpepper told Major Chaplin who stood and left the courtroom.

"The people call Mr. Coy Vanderveer to the stand."

"My roommate," Tagg told his attorney.

"And all he's got is that he owns a motorbike, right?" she ask her client.

"As far as I know."

The muscular man in his early thirties with a neat three days growth of beard and a trimmed mustache stepped through the courtroom doors at the bailiff's call. He wore a jacket and tie over jeans and polished boots and had a lip ring plus a half caret Cubic Zirconian stud in each ear lobe.

"Mr. Vanderveer," the D.A. addressed him once he was seated in the witness chair, "you share an apartment with the defendant, Mr. Tagg Truett, do you not?"

"I do."

"Are you friends?"

"I suppose. We've known each other since grade school."

"Do you own a lime green 2012 Kawasaki Ninja 250 R motor bike?"

"I do. I keep it in a storage locker out on E. American --- highway 84."

"U.S. 84, your Honor," Greason clarified.

"Does anybody else ride this dirt bike besides you?"

"It's not a dirt bike. It's a street bike."

"You don't ever take it off-road."

"Never. It doesn't have the tires for it."

"Again, does anyone else ride you motor bike besides you?"

"Not to my knowledge."

"Can you explain that answer, Mr. Vanderveer?"

"I'm kind of O.C.D. about my bike. I keep track of the mileage and change the oil and filters regularly --- just like with my truck."

"And?"

"Like I said, I keep it in a storage locker --- locked up --- but I do leave the keys in the bike. When I checked it last, there were about sixty something extra miles on it from the last time I used it."

The District Attorney walked over to the defense table before he asked his next question.

"Do you have more than one key to the lock on your storage unit?"

"Yeah. It's in my bedside table."

"Sixty extra miles. Would you happen to know how far it is from Clovis to Muleshoe?"

"Right at thirty miles it you go down to the light at the major intersection."

"Thank you, Mr. Vanderveer. Your witness," Greason said to Ms. Osburn.

"Let's examine your relationship with your roommate, shall we?" Roberta said.#

29

"First of all, Mr. Vanderveer, you say you have known my client since grade school," Roberta Osburn said as she began her cross-examination. "You are now sharing an apartment. And yet you didn't use the word 'friend' to describe your relationship."

"No, ma'am," the long haul trucker said. "We never were very chummy. I mean, we didn't dislike each other --- but we were just never buddy buddy, if you know what I mean."

"Oh, I do. There are a lot of people all of us know whom we would perhaps call acquaintances --- and even roommates if we shared living quarters --- but they're really not on the same wave length as us. We don't hang out together...."

"Your Honor, is the attorney for the defense testifying or is she questioning the witness?"

"There is a question in there somewhere isn't there, Ms. Osburn?" the judge said.

"Yes, and the question is, do you consider your roommate a friend?"

"Well, he's not an enemy? We don't dislike each other?"

"You are acquaintances --- roommates."

"Yes."

"You don't hang out together?"

"I'm on the road most of the time. He works nights --- we've seen a couple of football games together on TV --- but that's about it."

"So if the authorities asked my client if one of his *friends* owned a motor bike and he said, 'no,' would he be lying?"

"If he were thinking about me --- I guess not."

"Good, let's move on.

"This motor bike of yours --- have you ever invited your room-mate to go riding on it with you?"

"No. He's not into that kind of thing --- I think because of his leg."

"Have you ever taught him how to ride your vehicle?"

"Nope. He never asked."

"And the second key to your storage locker --- the one you keep in your bedside table --- have you checked on it?"

"I did after the sheriff asked me about it."

"Was it where you had left it?"

"Yes. It doesn't look like it's been moved to me."

"Thank you Mr. Vanderveer. No further questions." Roberta headed back towards her table.

"Redirect, your Honor," the D.A. said. "Mr. Vanderveer, if someone had used your key, could they have replaced it exactly where you left it so it would appear to be undisturbed?"

"Objection! Calls for speculation on the part of the witness, your Honor," Roberta shot back without sitting.

"Sustained," Judge Kulpepper ruled.

Fisher Marsh, a sixty-four year old crime scene forensic tech from the Clovis Sheriff's office was Greason's next witness. Marsh was a potato shaped little man with light brown hair, bushy eyebrows, bloodshot eyes, and a raspy voice.

Once he was sworn in and his credentials presented, the District Attorney asked, "Mr. Marsh, you examined the lime green 2012 Kawasaki Ninja 250 R motor bike from Mr. Vanderveer's storage shed did you not?"

"I did."

"Can you please tell us what evidence if any you recovered from this bike."

"The first thing to catch my eye was the sand burs."

"On a street bike?"

"Yes, sir. Sand burs of the genus *Cenchrus* and the family of Poaceae. The samples we found were still green --- telling me it wasn't but a few days old."

"How would something like this get on a machine which never was driven off road? And, yes, I am asking for speculation on the part of the witness whom I believed is well qualified to offer an opinion."

"Since I found multiple examples, I believe this bike had to be driven through an unmowed, unkept field with lot of high grass."

"Any other evidence?"

"A single thumbprint belonging to the defendant."

"How about the unaccounted for milage the bike's owner told us about? Would a trip from the storage shed across the state line to the edge of Muleshoe and back match that distance?"

"It would to within four tenths of a mile."

"No more questions," Greason said.

Roberta Osburn studied some papers on her desk before she rose and crossed to the witness.

"C.S.I. Marsh --- that's your official title isn't it?"

"Yes, it is."

"This sand bur you found on Mr. Vanderveer's motor bike, isn't it found in all the Americas, plus Africa, Asia, Australia and even on several islands around the world?"

"Yes."

"And have you ever discovered one on your slacks, socks, shirt, even your coat?"

"Rarely --- but yes. And usually when I've walked through tall grass."

"But not always?"

"There have been times when I've discovered them in my clothes and had no idea where they came from."

"Are you familiar with the West Texas wind, C.S.I. Marsh?"

"Of course."

"Do you believe it is possible for the West Texas wind to have blown sand burs on to you without your ever being in contact with any kind of vegetation?"

The C.S.I. didn't like having to answer this question.

"I'd have to say, yes."

"Very good," Roberta Osburn said.

"But ---."

"Next question Mr. Marsh."

"Your Honor, if the witness has more to say on this question, as an expert I believe the court deserves to hear it," the D.A. said.

"I agree," the judge nodded his head. "What were you going to say, C.S.I.?"

"The places I found these plants were hardly places the wind was likely to blow them. They were wedged in between mechanical parts of the bike which led me to believe they weren't picked up by the wind and just blown there."

"Have you ever found dirt or sand in the middle of your house, Mr. Marsh," Roberta asked, "which could have only come from the wind or the air conditioning --- which could be described as a form of wind?"

"Yes," the C.S.I. said as he slumped back in his chair.

"And driving a motorbike at sixty to seventy miles per hour might possibly drive a piece of vegetation deep into the mechanics of a speeding bike rushing through our West Texas wind, might it not?"

"Yes," he sighed. "However, the owner of the bike had been out of town for over a week and a half at the time we took possession of the bike."

"Let's move to another matter --- this thumb print. Where exactly was it found?"

"On the rear fender."

"Where on the rear fender?"

"Under the rear part of the seat near the exhaust."

The defense attorney went to the evidence table and picked up one of the photographs the C.S.I. had submitted.

"Here is the print you discovered, correct?"

"Yes."

Roberta looked at the picture a few moments, turning it to look at it from every angle. She brought the picture to the witness.

"Can you tell me how someone would have to be holding their hand in order to leave this print?"

The C.S.I. looked at the picture for a few moments and then twisted his hand around and around. He never could find a way to configure his hand. Ms. Osburn returned to her table where she picked up copies of the picture which she then handed over to the jury.

"Does make you wonder doesn't it?" she asked. "Oh, one last thing. That spare key in the bedside table. Did you fingerprint it?"

"Yes."

"Where there any prints on it besides the bike's owner?"

"No," the C.S.I. said reluctantly.

Roberta took her seat. "No more questions for this witness.

The judge called a lunch recess at that point.#

30

Friday afternoon in court saw D.A. Alfonzo Greason call his next witness, Sheriff Asa Hunt. The 69 year old, Bailey County Sheriff, all lean and leathered six feet six of him, looked like a Hollywood central casting character of a modern day rural Texas sheriff. His khaki uniform was starched --- he carried his cream colored Resistol straw hat and a bound folder in gnarled hands and had his engraved, Colt 1911 semi-automatic on his hip. After taking the oath he sat and turned his head so his good left ear was towards the D.A.

"Sheriff Hunt, can you please tell the court about the confrontation between the defendant and the deceased, Jarvis Dickle?"

Asa opened the folder on the ledge in front of him and put on his rimless bifocals.

"The incident occurred four and a half years ago," he said referring to the papers in the folder. "It was June 23rd, a hot and sticky night. A call came in at 9:07 P.M. of gunshots being fired around an old shed owned by Mrs. Maude Dickle. An ambulance and law enforcement was requested. I was in my unit headed home and I took the call myself."

"What did you discover when you arrived on scene?"

"There were two vehicles there --- Jarvis Dickle's '96 white Ford Ranger with a missing tailgate door and Tagg Truett's two year old red Dodge dually. On the ground beside the open door to the Dodge, Mr. Truett was lying on his side with a bloody t-shirt wrapped about his upper left leg and his butt."

"Where was Jarvis Dickle when you arrived?"

"Leaning up against the bed of his truck --- his .12 gauge was propped up on the ground beside him."

"What did the two men tell you had happened?"

Asa Hunt shut the folder. "Nothing. Jarvis had been the one who called in the incident and requested the ambulance. Tagg --- the defendant was screaming in pain ...."

Tagg leaped to his feet saying, "The asshole has just shot me in the ass with a .12 gauge!"

Judge Kulpepper began banging his gavel.

"Ms. Osburn restrain your client and have him mind his language in my court! One more word and I'll hold him in contempt and let him spend the night in jail!"

"He *is* in jail, your Honor," Roberta said grabbing Tagg and pulling him back to his chair, "--- but I apologize to the court."

Greason smiled at the outburst but controlled himself and turned back to his witness.

"Sheriff Hunt, did either man finally make a statement?"

"The defendant did say Jarvis had shot him, but when Jarvis asked Tagg to explain what he was doing, both men stopped talking."

"Did Mr. Dickle surrender his shotgun?"

"He did. He had already emptied the other shells in it into his truck bed."

"Can we assume an ambulance arrived soon."

"It did."

"You arrested Jarvis Dickle right then?"

"I did --- but when no charges were filed I had to release him."

"Mr. Dickle never went to jail for this?"

"No."

"How about the discharging shotgun."

"It's not against the law outside of city limits."

Alfonzo crossed back to his table and checked his notes.

"Oh, one last question, Sheriff. What, if any, was the relationship between the defendant and Jarvis Dickle at the time this shooting took place?"

"Tagg Truett was married to Jarvis Dickle's only daughter, Lottie," he nodded toward Lottie who sat with Maude and Caroline in the gallery.#

31

Lottie had been on the air Saturday morning since five A.M. A few minutes after nine she saw the reflection on the wall outside the control room indicating someone had opened the front door. She opened the door to find her boss, Webb "Wide-load" Fritz with another man and a girl about eight years old.

"Lottie, there you are," Webb said ushering the man and the child who clung to his hand forward. "Lottie Truett meet Calvin Dobbins."

"Cal," he said in a voice that sounded as if it came from the bottom of a deep well.

Lottie offered her hand as she adjusted to resonance of the voice. The man looked to be in his late thirties and had a close cropped beard covered pockmarked face. His warm expression of his perching hazel eyes shown past a long ago broken nose. He was just average height but had a full chest where the voice must have come from.

"Lottie," she said noticing how warm his hand was.

"And this is Phaedra Elaine," he said with a kindly hand ushering her forward.

The child had mousy brown hair the same color as her father's, but there was fire in her blue eyes and a timidness hiding an energy and intelligence which would not stay in the shadows.

"I'm glad she takes after her mother and not after me. My parents beat me with the ugly stick until it broke."

"Daddy always says that."

Lottie dropped to a squat and proffered a hand to the child, who after getting a nod from her father, stepped forward and gripped Lottie's palm, thumb to thumb. Lottie was both surprised and pleased.

"Phaedra. What a beautiful name. If I remember my Greek mythology, it means 'bright.'"

"It does," she said with a pleased expression. "But Mommie and Daddy got the name from a Nancy Sinatra/Lee Hazelwood song --- 'Some Velvet Morning.' Daddy says someday I'll understand it. I don't, yet. It's in the car and we play it all the time. I like 'These Boots Are Made For Walkin'.'"

"I do, too," Lottie said. "I play it sometimes just for myself."

"Elaine was my Mommie's name."

Lottie looked up at the child's father.

"Cancer," he said. "Little over a year ago."

"I'm so sorry," Lottie said to Phaedra.

"Thank you," the little girl said as if she was accustomed to people's sympathy.

Lottie stood as Webb spoke.

"Cal and Phaedra live in Dallas --- but they're looking to relocate. He's looking for a place to raise his daughter..."

"Somewhere where she can know the difference between city people and Texas people," he said almost hypnotizing Lottie with the wonderful voice " --- the difference between cows and crows."

"Muleshoe's that kind of place," Lottie smiled.

This man could never be a TV preacher or a politician. He didn't love the sound of his own voice enough --- although God knows he had reason enough to love it.

"He's also looking for a possible small radio station to buy," Webb finished his thought.

"It's just more expensive than I thought," Cal said.

"Well, even if you bought half of it, you'd own something in a good place to live."

"A half is about all I could afford."

"I didn't know you wanted to sell the station," Lottie said to her boss.

"Well, I'm not getting' any younger. Bella wants to take some cruises and do some traveling'."

"What are you asking?"

Webb told her.

"I'm just a big city announcer," Cal said. "Everything's more than I can afford, bet or borrow."

"Cal's been doing commercial announcing --- free-lance --- with several production companies in the Metroplex."

"Radio or voice over for TV," Cal clarified. "Everybody always said I had a the look for radio."

"You've certainly got the voice for it," Lottie said.

"Wish I could take some credit for it --- but I can't. The good Lord gave me this one talent."

"And a beautiful daughter," she said smiling at Phaedra.

Webb moved Cal past Lottie to show him the rest of the station.

"We're almost a one-man-band. We ride the network on A.M. and play country music on F.M. We do local news and the ag reports. That's what people around here care about."

Lottie studied this man for a few moments as they moved into the control room. She looked back at Cal's daughter and said to him, "Cal, are you a pretty good judge of character?"

The question surprised him.

"I've always thought so. Why?"

"I'm not always so good myself --- I know I've been fooled a time or too."

"Why do you ask?"

"What if you had a partner?"

"Huh?"

"Webb, if I could get a loan, I might be able to buy the part Cal can't afford."

"Are you serious?"

"Why not. This is all I know. Don't tell anybody, but Daddy left an insurance policy. I think I might be able to swing it --- if Cal is looking to partner up on the deal."

"Well, you know this includes my whole media empire, don't you?"

"Media empire?" Lottie asked.

"I also own The Stake," Webb turned to Cal. "The Muleshoe Stake --- it's a newspaper. And the Tribune in Friona."

"So if we bought in, we'd get two newspapers and the station?"

"Let's not kid anybody," Webb said, "this is a *local* radio station --- and two very *local* newspapers."

"That's the kind of thing I'm really looking for," Cal said. "I was a journalism major in college."

"Me, too," Lottie said.

"It's a big decision," Webb said.

"I'm ready to take a leap of faith," Cal responded.

"So am I," Lottie agreed.

The two new partners shook hands.

Lottie leaned down and picked up Phaedra.

"What do you think? What's your gut feeling, Phaedra Elaine?"

"I think we're moving to Muleshoe," she said with a big smile that revealed a couple of missing baby teeth.

"Then we're going to have to get you some boots. Everybody wears boots here."

In a matter of moments Lottie whole life had changed.#

32

Monday morning the first witness was a Rubenesque, large busted woman whose dress revealed plenty of cleavage. Her hair was raven black, cut in a page boy that looked too young for her 50 something years. This was Sobi Trejo who had for years run the local house of ill repute in Muleshoe.

When Alfonzo Greason asked her to state her profession she said, "Author." He asked her to be a little more explicit and she smiled.

"Being explicit is my stock and trade," she said. "I write erotica. One should always write about what you know. It's the first rule of writing."

"If it please the court," Greason said, "This witness has been granted immunity for her past --- shall we say 'indiscretions so that she may testify fully without having to rely on the Fifth Amendment against self-incrimination."

"I've read your brief, counselor, and while I don't condone your witness' --- let's say 'previous lifestyle' --- the court is willing to accept the agreement as long as no other significant felonies come to light."

"Understood, your Honor." To the witness the D.A. said, "Can you please tell the court what your previous profession was?"

"I owned and operated --- what I always considered an escort

service in Muleshoe. Others have less flattering --- even more tradi-
tional and derogatorily prejudicial names for my establishment ---
but whatever you might choose to call it --- the oldest profession has
that distinction because of the enduring need for my services."

"Your Honor," Roberta Osburn stood and said, "can't we call a
whorehouse a whorehouse?"

"For the record," Judge Kulpepper said, "I'd prefer not to. We're all
adults and understand what is being said. "Objection over ruled. The
prosecution may proceed."

"Thank you, your Honor."

Greason waddled back to his table and picked up a sheet of paper
before asking his next question.

"Ms. Trejo," are you familiar with the night the defendant was
wounded by the deceased?"

"You mean the night Jarvis Dickle shot Tagg Truett in the butt
with bird shot? Yes, I am."

"Were you involved in those events in anyway?"

"No, I was not."

Roberta got to her feet again.

"Objection, your Honor. If this witness has no connection to the
events in question, why are we listening to her testimony?"

"If it please the court," Greason said, "the relevance of her testimony will become clear momentarily."

"Proceed."

Ms. Osburn plopped down in her chair in disgust.

"Was a Miss Randy Piston in your employee at the time?"

"She was. And her real name was Megan Seeger."

"All right, what can you tell us about Miss Seeger?"

"She liked rough sex --- and Tagg Truett was a major client of
hers."

"I must object, your Honor. If this Miss Piston or Seeger --- whatever her real or working name was --- is material to this case, why are
we not hearing from her?"

"Miss Seeger is dead," Greason said.

"I'm so sorry to hear that," Roberta said with only a hint of sarcasm, "but then we are expected to listen to and accept hear-say, second hand evidence?"

"It's the best we can do," the D.A. said, "and the witness is not going to testify to anything she did not witness."

"Again, over ruled."

"Back to the night in question. Did you witness Miss Seeger leave your --- establishment --- with the defendant?"

"She met him. It was a regular appointment. Every Wednesday night."

Roberta stood once more.

"So, the witness never saw my client and her employee together?"

"No, I did not. But she told me where she was going and when she returned she told me with whom she had been."

The D.A. took over the questioning again without missing a beat.

"Why did Miss Seeger and the defendant not conduct their --- transaction --- in your establishment. Isn't that the way your business used to work?"

"It's known as an 'out call.' We did a lot of that kind of business in the motels and truck stops within an hour of home base."

"So, this was nothing unusual."

"No. In fact, their --- transaction -- was taking place off the premises because typically the noise of their --- business --- was very loud and even disturbing to other clients. For the sake of everyone involved, they had agreed to conduct their --- exchanges --- elsewhere."

"To make it clear. You knew Miss Seeger was going to meet the defendant in the old barn on the defendant's grandmother-in-law's property?"

"Yes. It was not used any more --- and I believe it offered the kind of atmosphere they liked."

"Speculation, your Honor," the defense attorney called out.

"The witness will restrict her remarks to what she personally saw and heard."

"Yes, your Honor," Sobi Trejo said.

"And when Miss Seeger returned?" Greason continued.

"She told me that she and the defendant were interrupted by Jarvis Dickle holding a shotgun."

"Hear say," Roberta said.

"How was Miss Seeger when you saw her after her '*out call*'?"

"Her clothes were torn --- she had rope burns on her hands and feet --- and marks from a belt or strap across her back. She was scared and bleeding."

"This wasn't what she and the defendant usually did when they were together?"

"No. She and he liked rough sex --- but this time it had gone way too far. I had always been afraid that was going to happen. It is my --- speculation --- my experienced guess --- that if Jarvis Dickle had not intervened when he did, Tagg might have killed Megan that night."

"Total speculation, your Honor. I ask that those remarks be stricken from the record."

"Objection sustained. Ms. Trejo since you were not there, you can't know for sure."

"I know what she looked like when she dragged herself back in. I know we had to take her to the emergency room that night --- and I know who inflicted those wounds on her."

"How do you know that?"

"She told the black sheriff's deputy who took her statement in the hospital."

"But she didn't press charges?"

"No. She saw Tagg come into the E.R. after he got shot, and she knew he had a tough go of it after that. Megan just didn't see the point. She said she thought she knew what she was getting into --- it just all went too far."

"Do you have anything else to tell us, Ms. Trejo?"

"Only that I closed my business the next day --- and I've never gone back to it. I never intended for anyone to get hurt. I took very good care of my girls --- medically and every other way. But I always told myself that the first time any of them were ever hurt, I'm out for good."

"And Miss Seeger."

"She went to nursing school --- I'm glad to say I helped her with her tuition. But remember when the doctor returned from Africa a couple of years back with ebola? Megan was the nurse assigned to his case --- and she caught it and she died horribly. The doctor survived --- but she didn't."#

33

Dallas flew in and took a cab to the Asian restaurant where Lottie, Maude, and Caroline joined him for lunch.

"What's the difference between Chinese and Tai food?" Maude asked looking at the menu.

"The spices they use in cooking. Chinese is soy sauce based. Thai food uses more fish sauce, basil, lemongrass, limes and peanuts. Thai is also usually more spicey. It has many different curries in it. Chinese tends to be greasier."

Maude put her menu down and studied her friend.

"Aren't you just a walking encyclopedia?"

"Spend as much time in a chair like I do and you spend a lot of time on line. You read --- you learn."

"I always wondered," Dallas said, "but I never knew who to ask."

"Google or Bing," Caroline said.

"Are you finished for the day?" Lottie asked Dallas.

"Yep. Only had one job this morning."

"Then you'll be able to hear the closing arguments after lunch."

"Is it that close to being done?"

Maude laughed, "You missed a real show before we broke for lunch. Roberta got her butt handed to her on a feminist platter."

"How so?" Dallas asked.

"Sobi Trejo was the last witness."

Dallas and Lottie exchanged looks but neither said anything.

"She admitted up front that she had been," Maude turned to Caroline, "--- what did she call it?"

"A sex worker."

"Right. A sex worker. Well, Roberta tried to rip her a new one for being a madame. Sobi gave it right back to her --- 'Doesn't a woman have the right to decide how to live her own life --- what to do with her own body?' All the arguments Roberta has been championing all these years."

"Nobody ever asked Roberta to be a sex worker, I'll bet," Caroline smiled. "I'll bet she was really pissed because of that deep down."

"I wouldn't doubt it," Maude said. "And all the other main feminist party line talking points she threw back in Roberta's face must have really stung."

"But you have to hand it to Roberta," Lottie said, "she didn't let her own opinions and beliefs get in the way of her doing her job."

"Not that it did much good. In the end I don't think she scored a single point," Caroline agreed with Maude.

"And that's 'cause *scoring* is something Sobi knows more about than Roberta ever will," Maude responded.

The whole table laughed at that.

After they had ordered and the table was quiet, Lottie spoke up.

"I have an announcement to make."

"We already know, hon," Maude said reaching over and patting Dallas' hand.

"It's not that," Lottie said.

"Tell us," Caroline said.

"I'm buying half interest in the radio station and two newspapers."

"The Stake?" Maude asked.

"And the Gazette in Friona. It was all part of Webb's media empire."

"And he's agreed to sell you half of it?" Dallas was surprised but not displeased. "I never thought he'd let go of it."

"Not just half. I have a partner. We're going fifty-fifty on the whole deal."

"Who?" Maude asked.

"Someone none of you have met, yet. His name is Cal Dobbins. God, you'll just love his voice. He's a voice over announcer from Dallas --- a widower with an eight year old daughter. He lost has wife to cancer about a year ago and is looking for a place that's 'real' to raise his girl. Oh, and her name is Phaedra Elaine --- you're going to love her."

"When did you meet him?" Maude asked.

"Webb brought the two of them into the station Saturday morning while I was on the air."

"And you decided to go into partnership with him then and there?"

"Pretty much, Nana."

"How could you do that?" Dallas asked. "It took me months to get you to even go out on a date with me."

"I knew what you wanted," Lottie said. "And I wasn't interested --- at first. But I did come around."

"That you did," he said giving her a hug.

"And Webb owns The Stake and the Friona paper, too? He's sure kept that under his hat," Caroline said.

"I had no idea he was interested in selling until he walked in with Cal and Phaedra."

"So, I'm going to marry a media magnet?"

"Hardly a magnet --- but the moment I thought of it I knew it was right."

"And you have no questions about this --- Cal character?" Maude asked.

"It's a gamble. I know it. But he said he was willing to take a leap of faith and I decided I was, too."

"I'm proud of you, Lottie," Maude said taking her granddaughter's hand in hers.

Caroline joined in and took both their hands in hers.

"Me, too."

Everybody looked at Dallas.

"Well, of course I am," he said defensively. "Whatever Lottie wants is A-OK with me."

Their food arrived.

When everyone was digging in, Maude observed, "All we need to do now is to wrap this trial up and move on. I see great things ahead."

#

34

"The case before you is very simply put, a case of revenge being a dish best served cold."

Alfonzo Greason was now at his best. The walrus like Bailey and Parmer County District Attorney, hooked a thumb in each vest pocket as he displayed himself before the jury as self-confident as a gunfighter standing in the door of an old time Texas saloon. Occasionally he'd stroke his drooping mustaches and van dyke beard while letting a point he had made fully sink in.

"The defendant before you, a handsome if lazy young man, once had it all. He was married to the most desirable woman in two counties."

Lottie blushed and looked down while Dallas pulled her to him whispering, "He damn sure has that right."

This brought a smile to Lottie's pretty face.

"But that wasn't enough," Alfonzo continued. "Nothing has ever been enough for Tagg Truett. He was a philanderer --- with prostitutes --- and enjoyed not just dominating them but hurting them." This was one of those mustache stroking moments.

"When he was caught in the act of not just cheating on his wife --- but inflecting savage pain on the roped and restrained body of a young prostitute he frequented --- by his own father-in-law ....” The D.A. allowed that picture to fully paint itself in the mind of each jury member before he picked up the story, “ --- he thought only of himself and fled. Jarvis Dickle did what any Texan of honor would have done in similar circumstances --- he shot the two timing louse. But --- he didn’t shoot to kill --- he used a shotgun --- loaded with birdshot --- and instead of trying to blow the cheater’s head off --- which I’d have had a hard time prosecuting him for under the conditions --- instead this highly skilled former military sniper only shot Tagg Truett in the butt.

“He released the young woman and let her go while he called an ambulance for the low life he’d just shot. Jarvis Dickle could have let Tagg bleed to death right there --- but he didn’t. Not only did he call for medical help, he unloaded his shotgun, laid it across the bed of his truck and waited there to be arrested and likely even go to jail.

“Now, I ask you --- in this picture, who is the hero and who is the villain?”

Greason walked over to his white board and pointed to the spot where the shooting took place.

“This is where it happened. Here,” he pointed to another mark, “is when Tagg and Lottie were divorced and when Tagg left Muleshoe --- left Texas to take a job as a bartender for a strip bar in Clovis, New Mexico. But he was no longer the handsome seducer he once was. Now he walked with a limp because of the damage done to muscle and tissue.”

The prosecutor turned back to his white board, “Look at the years that passed before Jarvis was murdered. Is this not revenge served cold?”

The District Attorney turned around and lumbered over to his table where he checked his notes.

“It is this far, far point in time we need to look at now. The day of the murder. This murder took a lot of thought and planning --- but what else did the defendant have to do besides stew in his own guilt and misery for all the intervening years?

“When D-Day arrived, his roommate, a long haul trucker was

headed across country and Tagg Truett was alone --- free to carry out his plan.

"First of all he had likely made himself a copy of the storage locker key months in advance --- although there's no evidence to prove it," the D.A. held up his hand before Roberta Osburn could even open her mouth. "Maybe he didn't have a key made --- maybe he taught himself how to pick a lock --- but nevertheless he managed to get into that locker and get the lime green motor bike he took that rainy morning from Clovis to Muleshoe.

"One way to throw suspicion from himself was the clever way the killer made himself memorable on the motorbike on this highway --- cutting in front of a truck he had seen in town before --- a truck with New Mexico plates. Of course, he had a helmet on and so his face wouldn't be seen, but the lime green bike --- very memorable.

"After all these years, Tagg knew the work habits of his former father-in-law and knew the layout of the workshop and surrounding area. Somehow, once Jarvis Dickle opened the steel accordion doors of his shop and was heating up his furnace, the killer slipped in, picked up three muleshoe nails and a hammer. With a single blow he drove one nail into the brain of the unsuspecting farrier. This stunned him and he couldn't move. Quickly two more nails were driven into the victim's head and he collapsed to the floor --- his life fluid draining out on the cold concrete. The killer then wiped off his finger prints from the hammer and anything else he touched, climbed on the motorbike and made his escape through the tall grass and weeds behind the shop. He was getting away with it.

"That's when the package delivery truck drove down to the end of the paved parking lot and made a u-turn. That's when the driver saw Jarvis Dickle's body on the floor of his workshop. He also saw the lime green motorbike head Northwest back towards New Mexico.

"The deed was done --- Jarvis Dickle, the man who had ruined Tagg's life --- what there was of it --- was now dead.

"When the bike --- which Tagg first says he had access to and then told two sheriff's he didn't have --- was noticed by its real owner, there were about sixty miles unaccounted for --- sixty miles it would take to drive from Clovis to Muleshoe and back.

"And the clincher was --- the one thumbprint Tagg Truett forgot to get rid of --- which puts him in the storage shed and on that lime green bike."

Alfonzo Greason took his bulk over to the defense table and counted off on three fingers.

"Means, motive, and opportunity."

Back to the jury he said, "Jarvis Dickle was no jewel of a human being --- but he was a man who served his country without question when called --- and the P.T.S.D. he suffered from was beyond what any of us will ever comprehend. But he did not deserve to die at the hands of a heartless killer who cared for no one but himself.

"Ladies and gentlemen of the jury your course is clear. Find Tagg Truett guilty of the callous crime of murder in the first degree --- for surely there was never a more planned and thought out killing than this. For his cowardly act, he deserves what he has given --- death."

The D.A. looked each juror in the eye and then went back to his seat.

"Closing argument, Ms. Osburn," the judge said.

"Your Honor. The people have failed miserably to prove its case. The defense moves for a directed verdict of not guilty."#

35

E veryone in the court room was astounded with defense attorney Roberta Osburn's motion for a "directed verdict" of not guilty. On the bench Judge Seward Kulpepper was the only one who took the motion in stride.

"Motion denied, Ms. Osburn. Your closing argument, if you please."

Roberta took the judge's almost casual reaction to her tactic without flinching. Instead she heaved her bulk out of her chair and slowly approached the jury.

"For just a moment, I'd like each of you in the jury to imagine yourself as the person seated over at the defense table --- accused of capital murder --- your life now on the line --- and your fate in the hands of twelve strangers who have been presented with a very circumstantial, flimsy case with a great deal of conjecture but very few facts. Now, if you were the one sitting in that chair, how would you like your future --- even your existence --- to be weighed against mere *possibilities* --- *speculation* --- and what you happen to know are *misconceptions* and *half-truths*?

"Remember how as a child you were fascinated by shadow puppets someone made against a wall with their hands and fingers?

That's what this case is. It's really not a bird, an elephant, or a rabbit whose shadow you see on the wall. It's the cleaver manipulation of light and shadow. If you saw the hand gestures by themselves, you'd never imagine the image they'd produce under just the right kind of light.

"Have you ever mistaken an individual across the mall, in a parking lot, or at the fair for a well known friend or even a relative? But when you called this person's name and/or approached them you discovered it's not who you thought you saw at all?"

Roberta walked over and stood behind Tagg.

"Your mind can play tricks on you. The truth isn't always two plus two that equals four. Sometimes two and two make twenty-two --- it's all how you look at it."

She patted Tagg on the shoulder.

"My client did not take the stand and testify --- under our constitution he doesn't have to --- and as jurors it is your job *not* to read anything into that fact. Can you please remember that? I asked him not to testify because the prosecution's case was so weak I saw no reason for him to do so. That was my call, not his. So, when you're back in your jury room deliberating this case, remember that. And try to remember how you'd feel if you were the one in this chair."

The defense attorney walked over to stand in front of the jury without saying anything as a way of changing the subject.

"This is a terrible thing to say --- but it is the truth --- for all the heroic deeds Jarvis Dickle did on the battle field under enemy fire --- when he returned home --- he was the kind of man you'd cross the street to keep from having to encounter.

"Some of you will remember the old John Wayne - Jimmy Stewart movie, 'The Man Who Shot Liberty Valance.' Lee Marvin played the bad guy, Liberty Valance. Maybe you've seen it on TV. And perhaps you've heard the song by the same title that Gene Pitney wrote and recorded. There's a line in that song that says, 'When Liberty Valance walked around, all the men would step aside.' That's how it was with Jarvis Dickle.

"Okay, he had P.T.S.D. --- he had a severe case of it --- but that didn't give him a Constitutional right to be an asshole."

"The defense council will watch her language in my court," Judge Kulpepper said, "or she will find herself in contempt."

"I apologize, your Honor. And I apologize to the members of the jury --- but there's simply not another word that conveys the way people felt about Jarvis Dickle. It is a shame. He was a hero --- and an honorable man in spite of the way he acted --- and I agree with the prosecution that Jarvis Dickle did not deserve to be murdered."

Roberta paused here for a few moments and then went on.

"But someone did kill him. That someone, however, was not my client. It had been years since they had any contact. And contrary to what the D.A. would have you believe, Tagg Truett is not the kind of man who nursed a grudge and carefully planned a murder. Frankly, and I have to say this, my client is not smart enough to work something like this out. He's a cad, yes, a womanizer --- he works as a bartender in a strip bar in Clovis. He happens to get off on rough sex --- so did the prostitute he was with the night he was shot by his then father-in-law --- and perhaps things got out of hand in that barn. But you add all of that up and it doesn't make him a murderer.

"I'm not asking you to like Tagg Truett --- maybe you'd even cross the street so you didn't have to cross paths with him --- but he is not a killer. He had moved on with his life. He didn't press charges against Jarvis Dickle for assault with a deadly weapon --- something most of us would have most likely done. He knew he was in the wrong that night --- and he took his punishment like a man. He lost his wife --- and now being a bartender in a strip bar is probably all he'll ever do. Still --- doesn't make him a killer.

"Look in your hearts and be honest with yourselves. Just because Tagg Truett isn't somebody you might like --- the evidence for the prosecution is a house of cards --- it's shadows on the wall --- the so called *facts* are all happenstance, circumstance, conjecture --- not proof.

"Isn't there a *reasonable doubt* in your mind that this man --- isn't who the state wants you to believe he is. Look at this from another angle --- in a different light --- the *facts* aren't very factual. They're not enough to cost a man his life for something he didn't do."

She walked back to Tagg and stood behind him once more.

"Remember --- what if it were you in this chair. Would you think there was enough evidence to convict? Of course not.

"Please do your job --- with faith, honor, and careful judgement. The truth isn't always what we'd like for it to be --- but your job is to find that truth where ever it is and declare it for the sake of justice.

"Your Honor, the defense rests."#

36

Three hours later, the foreman of the jury read the verdict returned to him after the judge had seen it. He read, "We, the jury, find the defendant, Tagg Truett, guilty of the charge of capital murder in the first degree."

"And your punishment?"

"Death."

Tagg sank down in his chair, but Roberta Osburn took him by the arm and helped him to get back to his feet.

"Tagg Truett," Judge Kulpepper said, "having been found guilty of the willful murder of Jarvis Dickle in the first degree, I hereby sentence you to death by lethal injection at a time and date to be set after the mandatory appeal."

Turning to the jury, the judge said, "Thank you, ladies and gentlemen, for your time and your service." He rapped his gavel and stated, "This court is adjourned."

Before Tagg could weaken again, two bailiffs were there at his sides to cuff him, hand and foot.

It didn't seem to be real as Lottie stood with Dallas, Maude, and Caroline.

"I told you we were likely to lose the first time," Roberta said to

Tagg. "Remember, I told you it's not over --- not by a damn sight. We now know the prosecution's game plan --- and we'll be ready for them next time."

"When?" Tagg managed to say above a whisper.

"Soon. I'm going to file briefs this afternoon to have the verdict overturned and demand a new trial."

The bailiffs now had Tagg secured and were ready to take him away.

"Just a moment," Roberta said to the pair. "Tagg, look at me. Tagg! This will not stand. I won't let it. I still believe in you --- and before I'm through with them, the judicial system will issue you a full apology and we'll sue their asses for false arrest and imprisonment. You keep that in mind."

The court officers shuffled Tagg away between them as the last of the jury disappeared through their door to the courtroom.

Lottie and her group still hadn't moved as the other spectators filed out and the District Attorney packed up and readied to leave. Greason offered his hand to the defense attorney.

"Hell of a job, Roberta --- as usual."

"Go to hell, Alfonzo!" she said. "This is not a game! I've never thought this courtroom decorum-for-attorneys bull shit was anything but crap. If you don't know this boy didn't do it, then you're dumber than I thought --- which I didn't think was possible. Next time we do this little dance, I'll kick your ass."

"I'm sorry you feel that way," he said calmly. Greason pushed through the swinging rail gate and left. Roberta turned back to her table and stuffed her papers into her battered old briefcase.

Lottie stepped up to Roberta with her cell phone recording. "Ms. Osburn?" Lottie asked.

Roberta turned with fire still in her eyes, saw the phone and opened her mouth to speak when she recognized Lottie. Her whole countenance changed.

"You're reporting on this, too."

"We're a small station."

"I'm sorry for what happened to your daddy and for what I said about him --- although we both know it was true. I don't have any comment except to say we will appeal this trial and this verdict."

"Thank you," Lottie said.

Dallas put his arm around her shoulder and ushered her out behind Maude and Caroline who slowly navigated her walker through the open doors.

THE NEXT THING Lottie knew they were sitting in a restaurant somewhere in town, but she had no idea which one or where.

"Do you want something stronger, Hon?" Maude asked her granddaughter.

Lottie noticed there was a Dr. Pepper in front of her. She made herself take a sip and shake her head.

"Are you going to be all right to drive?" Dallas asked rubbing one hand up and down the arm nearest to him.

"Yeah," she managed. "It's just --- so unreal."

"At least it's over," Caroline said.

"No, it's not. Didn't you hear Roberta? She's going to appeal. There will be another trial."

"Nothing says you have to go to it," Dallas offered.

"He's right," Maude said. "We weren't called to testify." She took a drink of her iced tea before saying, "I'm not sure I want to do this again."

"Do you really think Tagg did it?" Lottie asked.

"The jury thought so," Dallas said wrinkling his forehead. "You don't?"

"Roberta ---" Lottie started.

"Like I said, if I'm ever in trouble I want her as my lawyer --- she's damn good --- but, Hon, the Sheriff --- hell, two sheriffs, the D.A. and the jury all thought he did it."

"Who else is there?" Caroline asked.

"I don't know," Lottie had to admit.

"Unless we can find someone else," Dallas said, "--- this is the way our system works. And I agree, if anybody can get him off, it would be Roberta Osburn."

"Can't argue with that."

Maude reached across the table and took Lottie's left hand.

"This whole business has been a strain on all of us. I appreciate those motorcycle guys for what they told us about Jarvis, but Roberta was right about him, too. Liberty Valance --- Lee Marvin. Damn good analogy that movie. I'm sorry about my son --- your daddy --- but for whatever reasons he was who he was --- I wasn't surprised that some-body finally killed him."

Maude took hold of Lottie's engagement ring.

"You and Dallas have other things you need to be thinking about now. Remember, as soon as this trial was over ..."

Dallas smiled. "That's right. And there's your new business venture --- Ms. Media Magnet."

"When do we get to meet your new business partner?" Caroline asked.

"He has to sell his house in Dallas --- but I think he wants to get his daughter in school up here as soon as he can. So, a couple of weeks, I guess."

"Then he may come in while we're on our honeymoon."

"We'll make both of them welcome," Maude said patting Lottie's hand.#

37

L   ottie took Dallas out to the airport while Maude and
        Caroline checked out of the extended stay motel. They were
        ready by the time Lottie arrived back, and the three women
set off for Muleshoe down Interstate 27 then Southwest on U.S. highway 60.

Maude and Caroline talked about the wedding plans while Lottie
got lost in her thoughts. She pictured Tagg sneaking up behind Jarvis
and driving nails in his head. It was just possible and she had to
accept it as the truth. She still didn't miss her father and certainly
hadn't missed Tagg since he got out of the hospital and left town for
Clovis. Lottie had taken care of the divorce paperwork but was so
humiliated each time she had to make a trip to her lawyer's office or
the courthouse. She thought everyone was watching and judging her
ever moment.

That had, she realized, been the pattern of her life.

"Dickle the pickle" or "Popsicle Dickle" kids had called her in
elementary school. When she began to develop in the fourth grade,
ahead of the other girls, she stood out again. By the time she was
fourteen it was obvious she was going be large breasted like her
grandmother.

Most people don't realize the unwanted attention that a more mature figure has on teenage girls. The especially well endowed have a burden not even suspected by the average girl, much less the boys --- not just the weight, the neck and back strain.

By the time she was sixteen, Lottie was her current 42 E. She knew she was going to wear the largest T-shirts made the rest of her life or spend time with needle and thread to close the gaps between front-button blouses with Velcro. Tank top, backless dresses, and swimming suits were never going to be her friends. Going up or down stairs always drew attention and she didn't run anywhere. Without a waist she looked pregnant in any dress she wore. She did all her shopping on-line --- items delivered in plain brown wrapped packages. She even had to sleep in a bra.

As she drove home, the shoulder strap of the seat belt dug into her neck as per usual.

It was a different life being so busty than everyone else imagined. She realized that all girls were almost as curious as the boys --- and while the boys couldn't tell you what color her eyes were --- the girls were all jealous. If they only understood.

In high school her nick names were "Tickle her nipples" or "Dickle my pickle." By the time she want to Texas Tech for college, she was used to people *accidentally* bumping into her and copping a feel --- even women. When she was around, the conversation always seemed to turn sexual. When she wasn't as flirty or cosy with the boys as expected, the word became "The Obstacle is Dickle."

She gravitated to radio even though her professors and friends all wanted her to try TV.

One of the things about Tagg was that he was an ass man --- such a contrast to most of the guys she tried to date. And, now that she thought about it, she never once had to tell Dallas, "Hey, look up here."

Another thing, as she thought about it, Tagg and Dallas had in common --- they didn't obsess about her breasts. Dallas very much enjoyed her boobs, but she never caught him looking at them instead of at her.

But Tagg a killer? She never did know him. She did figure out he was playing around on her early on --- but once they were married, she either had to live with it or have a confrontation she knew would end only in divorce. So she avoided it at all costs.

After Jarvis had shot Tagg, there was no getting around it. They had the confrontation one day when his pain killers were wearing off --- and what she had expected was ten times worse. Screaming at each other until the hospital staff made a crying Lottie leave.

He signed the paper in his bar --- the stale smell of beer and cigarette smoke hit her like a fist when she opened the envelope he mailed back to her.

"You're going to miss the turn," Maude said breaking into Lottie's thoughts.

"Oh," she said and made the sharp turn down South Texas highway 214 in Friona.

"Where were you?" Maude asked.

"Just thinking."

"About?"

"Tagg --- and me --- and Daddy."

"How about focusing on your wedding?"

"Good idea," Lottie admitted.

Caroline asked, "Dallas never made a big deal about not having the wedding at the Methodist church?"

"No. His mother didn't care either. I don't think she's going to show up. But he hasn't said that, yet."

"I hope you're as happy with your dress as I am," Maude said. "I was afraid we were going to have to have one made."

"That's part of what I was thinking about. How hard it is to find anything that fits."

"Goes with the boobs, hon."

"I know, Nana."

⌇

"I UNDERSTAND MAJOR MAJOR," Tagg told Alberta in the interview room. He was back in Muleshoe having been transported by Texas Rangers to the Bailey County Jail where he had spent his first night under arrest.

"Catch Twenty-two," his attorney nodded her understanding.

"Anything that makes time go slower makes life last longer."

"Is that your philosophy now?"

"Sort of. Thanks to you --- and all the time I have on my hands, I've found I enjoy reading --- something I thought I was finished with when I left high school. By the way, thanks for the books."

"Let me know when you're ready for some more and I'll get them."

"What's the plan? Do I stay here?"

"No. Since the trial is over and we're awaiting an appeal date, they're going to move you to Huntsville in a couple of days."

"With all the real killers."

"It might help you to play it like you're one, too. Murderers have high status there. And everybody says their innocent, so don't waste your time trying to convince anyone."

"Got it."

"You seem to be doing a lot better than you were a couple of days ago."

"When I'm not reading, I've been thinking --- and I've decided to leave it in your hands."

"Good decision."

Tagg had thought about what he said next and took a moment before he said the words.

"You've done better by me than I probably would have done if things were reversed. You know that, don't you?"

"I figured it out. Lesbians are not your thing."

"Just stupid predjudists on my part. More than a few of the strip-pers I work with are lesbians. Some of them, like everybody else, are good people. I just never gave them a chance."

"Unless they gave you what you wanted."

Tagg had to laugh.

"You have figured me out."

"It's not that hard."

"Hell, I could be a lessie. I like women."

"You don't have the equipment."

"I used to think --- look down between your legs --- whatever's there is what you are."

"Some of us ended up with the wrong attachments."

"I still don't understand men on men. Women on women --- I can see the attraction."

"It's more basic than that. It's something we can't control."

"I'm starting' t' get it. Well --- on behalf of all us asses --- sorry. I didn't choose to be straight --- and I don't think you decided one day you were going to swing the way you do. Now, I believe we are born to be whatever we are. And folks like you --- well --- you've got a hard row to hoe."

"And more than a few of us decide the only way to make it is to be a ho."

Tagg laughed in spite of himself and Roberta laughed with him.#

38

Tagg's head exploded like a watermelon hit by a wrecking ball at full force. The two jail deputies slightly behind him with grip on each elbow and the pair of prison guards opening the back doors to the prison transport van were all splattered with brains and blood. For a moment his body remained standing without his head --- then it collapsed to the sidewalk before it tipped over on its right side.

The stunned lawmen couldn't register what had just occurred. This all happened on the sidewalk from the jail end of the Bailey County Sheriff's Office to the parking lot. When they did, they all dropped to their knees and pulled their pistols scanning in different directions in the slightly foggy morning. But there was no movement any of the men could detect. There was not even the report of a firearm being discharged.

Four blocks North on Avenue D, up the hill and past the elementary school, a washed out blue van began to roll down the hill the opposite direction, two wheels on the asphalt and two in the grass. When it had reached about ten miles per hour, the clutch was popped and the engine turned over quietly with a slight jerk. At the next corner it turned left on West 6th and was gone.

Later, Mrs. Benavides would recall seeing the van parked there when she had gone to get her morning paper, but thought the Nava's son was in town from his rough necking job in the Gulf. She didn't get any license plate number nor could she even tell the make of the vehicle. All she remembered was that it had dark bubble windows on the rear, but one of them was missing.

Back at the Sheriff's Office, the deputies and the prison guards had stayed put and called the dispatcher to report the crime without taking any more steps than were necessary. They all knew the importance of preserving the crime scene.

"Prisoner down! Repeat! Prisoner down! East end of the jail!"

Lottie was on the air when she heard the deputy call the dispatcher. "Prisoner down" could only mean one thing. She whipped around in her chair and located Marty Robbin's "El Paso" and slipped it in one of the CD players.

In almost the same motion she grabbed the phone and called Simon Ohlendorf's cell phone. The teenager answered on the second ring.

"Lottie? What's up?"

"There something happening at the Sheriff's Office. I need you on the air --- right now!"

"I'm just parking my truck at school."

"Good. Don't even turn off the engine. You've got four minutes and sixteen seconds to get here --- starting now."

Lottie pressed the play button on the CD player and ran the slider up on the audio board.

In his truck Simon heard the song began to play over his radio.

"I'm going out the door. Call Webb and tell him after you get here."

"Yes, ma'am."

LOTTIE PULLED up and parked across the street in the County Courthouse lot. The blank white prisoner van was parked with doors open to the jail and an ambulance arrived just as she did.

Deputies were stringing yellow Crime Scene ribbon around the van and the East end of the jail. Within another few moments Chief of police Luis Elizondo was on the scene with two of his patrol cars. He got out and approached Sheriff Asa Hunt.

This jurisdiction of this killing was a little vague. Clearly it happened in the city limits and so fell under authority of the stout, thin mustache, Chief Luis Elizondo. But it happened on the property of the County Sheriff, so the 45 year old Chief of local police said he thought it should be a joint operation. Elizondo ran a hand through his thick, combed straight back hair, when Asa disagreed.

"To keep this clean," Asa said, "it either should be your show or at least your lead."

"Want me to call in the Rangers, too?"

"That's not a bad idea," the older man said. "I don't want there to be any question about how this was handled."

"Ten-four," Chief Elizondo said.

Lottie saw a body covered with a tarp --- but it was misshapen. There was no protrusion where the head should be.

"Is that Tagg?" she asked one of the deputies who started to speak and then stopped when he recognized Lottie. He still didn't speak. He just nodded his head and went back to stringing the Crime Scene tape.

It was a good half hour before Lottie could get Asa to speak to her. All he would tell her was to confirm that the body on the ground was Tagg's and that his head had been blown off.

She phoned that report in and Simon put her on the air over the phone from the scene. It was a struggle for Lottie to remain professional, but she managed to do so by keeping the report short. She promised listeners she would report more details when they were available.

But even with the Texas Rangers lending their guidance, resources and expertise, after three days the mysterious faded blue van was the only major lead. The slug had been recovered from the rock and concrete back wall of the building backing up to the Sheriff's end parking lot. It was so distorted and deformed the only information that could be gathered from it was that it was a .30-06. No rifling marks could be identified.

Naturally the first suspects were the Texas Rebel Snipers. But the group was fully accounted for on a ride along the Blue Ridge Mountains. Not a member or a rider was missing or unaccounted for over the last week. Video footage from filling stations, bars and restaurants from Houston to Georgia and up to Pennsylvania were the eye witness evidence.#

39

"Do you want to put off the wedding --- at least a couple of weeks?"

Dallas and Lottie were in bed but hadn't made a move. Neither of them seemed to feel like it.

Lottie turned to Dallas with her mouth open.

"You'd do that?"

"My love, this all about you. Since Tagg was killed, I know everything's been really messed up in your head."

"That's putting it very kindly."

"There is a killer amongst us."

"Amongst?"

"I'm trying to sound educated."

"Which you are."

"Thank you. So, where is the investigation? Still nowhere?"

"From what I can find out."

"That was a hell of a shot. Downhill --- almost half a mile away. I'm good but I'm not *that* good. I would have thought it was one of the sniper bikers."

"The Rangers thought that, too. Turns out they're all riding the Blue Ridge Mountains."

"Just taking in the fall colors?"

"That was my question. Those days are past."

"Anybody thought about it being a pro?"

"A hitman?"

"Or woman. Let's not be sexist."

"If they're looking into that, they're not saying."

"So, I'll take that as a 'yes' --- about postponing?"

Lottie kissed him.

"Thank you. I didn't want to ask."

"Why not? Haven't I waited a couple of years already? What's a little while later? I'll call the church tomorrow."

"I'll call the rest. Thank you, Dallas."

"Anything for you."

"Well, I'm planning a little surprise for you. I hope you'll like it. You might think it's a little strange...."

"Strange can be good. Does it involve hookers and my bachelor party?"

She slapped him on the arm.

"It certainly does not!"

"I should have known that."

"Yes, you should," she turned her back to him and pouted.

"I was just kidding, Lottie."

After a moment she turned back to him smiling.

"I know you were. I'm sorry I get so touchy."

He stroked her arm.

"I happen to like touching you --- very much."

They kissed again.

"Oh, can you come down to the station tomorrow? Cal Dobbins and his daughter will be here. Their house sold quicker than they expected."

"I believe I can handle that. But what do I say to the preacher? Do we have a time table or ...."

"Why don't we say --- two --- make it three weeks. I mean, there's nothing we can change about what's happened --- and I do want us to start our new life."

"Me, too."

"One more thing, Dallas."

"Name it."

"I'm so wrung out --- do you mind if we --- just sleep tonight?"

"Only if I get to hold you."

"You do." She kissed him again.

CAL AND PHAEDRA came in a little before noon. Lottie was still on the air and Webb was preparing his noon newscast. The two men talked while Phaedra looked through the window and watched Lottie work.

Wideload stepped into the control room with the news copy in his hand as the last song was playing. Lottie got out of the chair and waved to Phaedra while she played a commercial. When it ended, she pulled the mic over to herself and clicked it on. Lottie gave a station I.D. and started the prerecorded noon news intro.

Webb pulled the mic toward himself as the intro played and Lottie exited the room.

"Look at my boots, "Phaedra said as soon as Lottie cleared the second door of the sound lock between the control room and the hallway. The child stuck out one foot to display her shiny new footwear and then did a little Hokey Pokey step and stuck out her other foot.

"You look just like a cowgirl," Lottie said opening her arms and letting Phaedra rush into them. "You're going to fit right in."

Dallas pushed his way through the front door. Lottie spun Phaedra around and put her down.

"Cal," she said to a beaming man a few feet away, "this is my fiancé, Dallas Kerkendall."

The younger man offered his hand to Cal.

"Pleased to meet you," Cal said. "And here I thought we were leaving Dallas behind."

"Good one," Dallas laughed. "My pleasure, Cal. Welcome to Muleshoe."

"Where are you staying?" Lottie asked.

"Nowhere yet. I'm looking for a motel --- but I thought we'd do lunch first."

"First lesson," Lottie said, "we don't *do* lunch here, we *eat* it."

"Ah," Cal said nodding. "We're not in the fake world any more. It'll take me a while."

"I see what Lottie meant about your voice, Cal," Dallas said. "Whoa."

"Wish I could take credit and say, 'Thank you,' --- but it's a gift. I didn't ask for it, I certainly haven't done anything to deserve it."

"Oh, I get it. It's kind of like my ability to fly. I was as surprised as anybody --- but my dad owned the crop-dusting business and liked to say it was in my genes."

"Dallas is a local legend. In high school, five touchdowns in a single game," Lottie said taking his arm.

"Yeah, I'm a real Al Bundy."

"I was first string AV," Cal said. "and chess club."

They all laughed.

Dallas said, "We all had to be somewhere. We had some guys who played in the band at half time but were on the team, too."

"Why don't you and Phaedra stay out at the ranch," Lottie said. "Nana has plenty of room, and she'd love to have you."

"Are you sure?" Cal asked.

"Trust me. Let's go eat. After we do that, we can go scuff up those new boots a little." Lottie looked down at Phaedra, "Ever ride a horse?"#

40

I n the days and weeks that followed, there was no news from
authorities about Tagg's murder.

Lottie and Cal Dobbins officially took over ownership of the
radio station and the newspapers. Phaedra got started in school in the
third grade. Cal's payout from everything in Dallas was larger than he
expected. With the extra he bought the Burley Keiber ranch right
behind the Dickle place. This was the same ranch Maude had used
years ago to avoid being arrested by Asa Hunt after she had been
caught peeing on a Muleshoe city limit sign.

Maude made a deal with Cal to use her property to run some
cattle of his own. She was tired of seeing her place go to seed since
her husband Jasper had died years ago. Cal hired a ranch manager
and soon there was real life growing and thriving again.

Gloria Clift, the florid, wrinkled skinned widow of the late
preacher at the Baptist church, took on the task of wedding planner.
By the time the day arrived, the widow had pulled everything
together and the ceremony was a success. All the church ladies who
had been the first to Maude's house after Jarvis' murder were behind
the scenes seeing that the event flowed without a hitch.

Lottie's off white, almost cream colored floor length gown was lovely. Covered with lace and pearls it couldn't diminish Lottie's dynamic figure but without any opening for cleavage or leg, it could best be described as a modest and understated dress. Dallas stood straight and tall in his Western tux and polished boots.

The surprise was the wedding ring Lottie had for Dallas. He didn't expect one and was taken aback for a moment before offering his left hand to Lottie. She slipped the engraved circular band on his ring finger.

They had the reception in the fellowship hall and a pianist and harpist provided the music. Dallas didn't even lobby for his band, the Staked Planes, because weddings weren't ever the kind of crowds they played for.

When they were ready to leave, the couple hurried down the steps through a shower of bird seed and bubbles blown by kids to Dallas' waiting truck. Lottie paused, faced away from the crowd and pitched her bouquet into the group of single girls who waited eagerly.

Dallas helped Lottie into the decorated truck and rushed around to the driver's seat. They moved off to the cacophony of clanking tin and aluminum cans tied to the trailer hitch. Someone had also seen fit to attached a small blue bag with what appeared to be the testicles of a stallion below the hitch. It's swinging as the newlyweds drove off brought a laugh from everyone.

Dallas turned left so they would go behind the County Court house instead of straight past the site were Tagg had been killed beside the Sheriff's Office.

In Lottie's duplex, Dallas changed out of the tux while Lottie slipped out of her gown. Her open suitcase sat on one end of the bed. They both changed into jeans to travel.

"Which one of your guys is going to clean up the truck?" Lottie asked as she pulled off her pantie hose and pulled on socks.

"I didn't trust any of them. They all still think we're driving somewhere. I got your new partner to pick it up in about an hour at the hanger and give it a good wash."

"Cal? I'm so glad you two are getting along. I think he's a nice guy."

"Not much to look at, but he seems like a straight shooter."

"That acne he had as a teenager must have been terrible."

"Must have been."

Dallas was dressed while Lottie, in bra, panties and socks, pulled on her T-shirt and reached for the jeans in the suitcase. He examined the ring and pulled it off to read the engraving inside.

"Today's date? I guess I have no reason to ever forget an anniversary."

"That's the plan."

"Neat pattern. Who made it?"

"A jeweler in Amarillo. I gave him the gold and he melted it down to make the ring. Of course he had to redo the date when we changed it."

"Well, as long as it's right."

"Where did the gold come from?" he asked slipping it back on.

Lottie tucked her shirt into her jeans and zipped them closed.

"It's been in the family for a few generations. Originally it was a brooch from my great grandmother. She gave it to my Aunt Loretta. After she died and left it to Nana, she had it melted down and turned into a wedding ring for my grandfather, Jasper. It ended up being a ring for Daddy that he quit wearing after mother died."

She was stepping into her boots while the expression on Dallas' face completely changed. He pulled it off his finger and almost snarled, "This was a ring that Jarvis wore?"

Lottie was caught off guard by the abrupt change in his tone. She had one boot on when she looked up and didn't recognize the appearance of the man she had just married.

"What's wrong? It's not his ring --- it's some of the same gold --- but it is a brand new ring."

Dallas ground his teeth together and threw the metal circle at her face. It hit her right cheek just below her eye and cut her skin before clanging off the wall over the headboard of the bed and landing on the floor behind her under the window.

"Ow!! Dallas! What are you doing? You don't like it?"

"You expect me to wear something that Jarvis wore? And you want me to always have it on my hand? I didn't want his guns, I didn't want his money --- why in hell would I want this ring?"

Lottie dabbed at her cheek with her hand and saw blood come away on her fingers.

"You did want his daughter. Dallas, what's going on?"

"You just don't get it, do you! Do you know why my mother wasn't there tonight?"

"I asked you and you wouldn't say."

"She dead. She's been dead for two years."

"Why didn't you ever say anything?"

"Because it was Jarvis that killed her."

"How?"

"Not only didn't you know him, you couldn't even guess who he really was."

Again Lottie dabbed the blood on her cheek. "So, tell me."

It took a moment for Dallas to gather his thoughts as his breathing picked up.

"Your father was having an affair with my mother --- he moved in after my dad died. He was sleeping with her while your mother was dying --- did you know that?"

"I don't believe it."

"Well, believe it. I had to put on head sets and crank up the volume whenever he came over to keep from thinking about what they were doing. Then when he came back --- he wouldn't even see Mom. He wouldn't talk to her on the phone. Piece of shit!"

Lottie's mouth dropped open.

"Do you have any idea what it took to get rid of him and blame it on Tagg?"

"What are you saying? You killed --- Daddy --- and Tagg?"

"I wasn't going to allow him to exist --- that ass hole, your father!

But do you have any idea how hard it is to kill one man and blame it on another one? Two birds with three nails?"

"Dallas! You killed them?"

"How many times do I have to tell you? Of course, I did!"

"Then we're through!" she yelled back at him.

Dallas back-handed Lottie across the other side of her face and she flew across the bed and tipped over her suitcase with her. She hit the wall and was stunned.

"No! We're just beginning! And I tell you one more thing, since I'm sure you don't understand it," Dallas roared! "You and I are married! You are my wife! *You* can't testify against me! Not that you're going to live that long."

Lottie snuck a hand into the overturned suitcase.

"When did you decide to do this? And how did you do it?"

"Picked a lock --- borrowed a street bike --- went to a certain Clovis strip bar and stole a glass with the bartender's fingerprints on it! That and a lot of thought."

A raging Dallas heaved the bed out of the way exposing Lottie against the wall in front of the suitcase.

"Come on, darlin'. We have one last trip to take. We have a Beechcraft waiting for us out at the hanger. It will be a shame when you fall out of it at few thousand feet high."

He stepped over the bed and leaned down toward Lottie.

"Then a month or so from now, there's going to be a fire at the Dickle ranch one night."

He grabbed her by the T-shirt, his fingers looping under her bra straps as he pulled her up.

Lottie had managed to locate her vest and worked her way to the inside pocket. She fired the pistol through the garment. Dallas froze. She fired twice more and he dropped her and fell across the bed, knocking the bedside lamp off while starring with dead eyes at the ceiling.#

41

Lottie was dressed with both boots and her vest with the holes blown in it on as she sat on the living room couch. The front door was open and the first officer through the door was Emmett Longley --- lanky but muscular, he had been the first guy she had ever had sex with. That was years ago, after a football game under the bleachers. He had been the second chair trombonist at half time but wide-out on the field during the game. He was funny and smart but not ambitious. He couldn't keep his mouth shut about his conquest. Quickly Lottie's nickname was 'Dickle for a nickel.' After graduation he had gone into the Marines and since getting out, he had been a local cop.

He had his .40 caliber Glock held with both hands close to his face as he eased the door open with his foot.

"Lottie? It's Emmett Longley!"

"It's clear, Emmett. I'm on the couch. Dallas --- the bedroom."

The policeman eased into the duplex. The flashing lights from his car winked through the windows and through the open door.

Lottie's pistol was locked open, laying on its side, a round from the chamber was beside it and the magazine under the lamp on the table at the end of the couch.

The officer picked up Lottie's weapon and her magazine with one handkerchief covered hand then walked sideways into the bedroom. When Emmett saw Dallas, he stopped. After a deep breath, he stepped over and checked the body for a pulse in the throat. There was none.

Back in the living room, he put his pistol away as he said, "Tell me what happened."

Two weeks later to the day, Lottie got a call from Police Chief Luis Elizondo asking her to meet Sheriff Hunt and him at the Coffee Mug around nine A.M. She had been off the air since the shooting and was staying out at the ranch with Maude, Caroline, Cal, and Phaedra.

"What do you think about your ability to judge character, now?" she had asked Cal a few days after the shooting.

"I'll stick by my first call," he told her with a gentle smile.

Lottie had not been jailed --- even for a night --- and she called Roberta Osburn to be at her side from her first interview at the police station on. There had been two days of the same questions and answers --- the form of the questions differed from the police side but, as per Roberta's instructions --- Lottie kept saying the same thing --- almost word for word --- each time.

Then nothing. She wasn't called in any more and no one told her anything about the investigation. This meeting, as odd as it was to be held at the Coffee Mug, was her first contact with authorities in nearly a week and a half. Luis Elizondo promised her she didn't need Roberta but was welcome to have her along. Roberta was the very next call Lottie made.

When all four were gathered and seated in the back booth, a hush seemed to settle over the diner. Even after Inez Brinkley served them all the coffee they'd ordered, she kept cleaning the empty tables around them and refilling filled salt shakers.

"Inez," Asa finally said, "--- enough."

She put her hands on her hips and glared at the Sheriff.

"I am trying to keep my business clean --- if that's alright with you, Asa."

"It's fine with me, but how about giving some attention to some other tables for a while?"

Inez stalked off in huff.

"The reason we're doing this here, Lottie," the Chief said quietly, "is because we all know that what's said here doesn't remain here."

"What does that mean --- exactly," Roberta challenged.

"It's over," Luis said in his normal voice. "There aren't going to be any charges filed --- but for you sake, Lottie, Alfonzo Greason is going to ask for a 'no bill' from the next grand jury."

"Whenever the hell that happens to be," Roberta said.

"That's why we're doing this in precisely this way," the Chief said. "It could be six to nine months before there's anything else that requires a grand jury, and none of us want you sitting around waiting, Lottie, wondering what's going to happen. We're just jumping through the hoops so this can never come back on you."

Lottie nodded and Roberta agreed with a slight inclination of her head.

"Now, so you'll know what we know," Luis went on, "we found a freshly painted candy apple red van for Dallas' band in the second hanger."

"That's he favoriate color."

"Under the five to six coats on it now, there's a faded blue. The bubble windows in the back door have been replaced with flat glass. There are also some marks on the floor and the wall, under the carpet and the paneling where a rack, or rest, had been welded in place. A good place for a shooter to lay prone level with the missing window. We even recovered some GSR --- sorry, gunshot residue --- from the ceiling and the wall."

The Chief turned to Asa Hunt who had sat quietly so far. Now he leaned forward and said, "Behind the locker where Dallas kept his hunting rifle was another one --- a .30-06 with a scope and a custom made silencer. We figured he made it himself. One of my deputies located it."

The Chief of Police picked up the story again.

"We don't know how he got into the storage locker in Clovis and got the bike --- "

Lottie interrupted, "Remember his saying something about picking a lock?"

"That's what we figured but there's no way to prove it. We never found any lock picking tools. But we did find a rider's outfit, boots and a helmet. Under one of the arms of the jacket was a sand bur that matched those found on the bike."

"And Sheriff Ybarra told me," Asa spoke up again, "that after a closer look, Tagg's thumbprint doesn't seem to be natural. It's too clear and --- it looks planted."

"Bottom line," Roberta interjected, "Dallas was the perp and framed Tagg for Jarvis' murder."

"That's the way it looks," Luis said sitting back. "It was a good frame --- but a frame."

"And Lottie is exonerated on all levels," Roberta wrapped up. "Free and clear."

"That's it," the Chief said.

"When can she have her pistol back?"

The Chief produced the Sig Sauer .9 mil and slid it, and the magazine across the table to Lottie."

"There was a round in the chamber," Roberta said.

"It's in the mag."

The sound level of the diner eased up to normal within a few moments.

Lottie pocketed the pistol on one side and the magazine on the other.

"Thank you," she said after there was nothing else to say.

"We're all sorry for all the grief and pain this has caused you, Lottie," Asa said.

"He had me fooled, too," she said getting up. "I don't believe either the Sheriff's Office, the Police Department or the D.A. intentionally did anything wrong."

"Don't be so quick on that," Roberta said sliding out of the booth.

"You could change your mind later --- and there are grounds for infliction of mental distress and ...."

"No," Lottie cut her off. "It's over. I don't want to punish anyone."

"Well, I thought it was worth a shot," Roberta said with a shrug.

As they walked out, people said, "Hi" or "We were behind you all the way," to Lottie.

Outside, Asa held back as everyone got in their vehicles and pulled away. To Lottie Asa said, "This isn't for publication, yet --- but I'm going to step down."

"Because of this?"

"If I can be fooled this badly --- and get a man killed because of it --- well --- my time is done. There's a very sharp deputy who is ready to take over --- I think she can prove herself before the next election.

"Lottie, I am sorry about Jarvis. Whatever he was --- he was still your pa. And Dallas --- that's just a shame on every level."

"Thank you, Asa. I've always respected you --- and I still do."

"Then take some advice from this ol' man."

"I'm listening."

"No more football players. Look for someone in the band --- or a geek of some kind."

"Maybe if Emmett Longley wasn't married --- didn't have three kids. But I'm not going to be looking for anyone, Asa."

"Good plan. A good one will find you."

THE END#

2 Free Ebooks

ChroniclesMURDER IN MULESHOE
There's a killer in town. Do we hunt the S.O.B. down or throw him a parade?

GUNS ALONG THE RIO
Two fresh-off-the-ranch 17-year-olds join the Texas Rangers in 1858. What could possibly go wrong?

GO TO: http://eepurl.com/dKEi_Y

THANKS

Thank you for taking the time to read <u>Murder In Muleshoe</u> (Book 1 of The Texas Panhandle Murders). I hope you enjoyed it. If you did, please consider posting a short review online at the site where you purchased the book and telling your friends. Word of mouth is an author's best friend and is much appreciated. I love to write these stories, but it's even better to sell some and to know other people take some joy from them, too.

If you're interested in subscribing to my monthly newsletter, contact me at jacks@wrightbridgepress.com. You will know when my next novel is coming out and a little bit about how I work. I would love to hear from you.

Thank you,
    Jack R. Stanley

ABOUT THE AUTHOR

Jack R. Stanley is an award winning novelist, playwright, and screenwriter. As an officer and combat photographer in Vietnam he earned the Bronze Star. Yet he says, "When you're in a firefight and everybody else on both side have guns while you have a camera --- you get to change your pants a lot."

After his military service he received both his M.A. and his Ph.D. at the University of Michigan in Ann Arbor in Radio-TV-Film. His doctoral dissertation was on the long running TV series GUNSMOKE. Stanley also received two of Michigan's most prestigious creative writing awards, The Hopwood Award, one for a one-act play and the second for a novel.

Still married to his gifted high school sweetheart, Stanley's first academic position was TV Area Head at The University of Texas at Austin's Department of Radio-TV-Film. He later moved to deep-south Texas and the Lower Rio Grande Valley for a challenging position with The University of Texas-Pan American. Here he taught Theatre-TV-Film for 30 years in the Department of Communication serving as Department Chair at U.T.P.A. for 11 years. He did take one year out to work for The University of Alaska Anchorage as a visiting professor. Back in Texas, Stanley directed for stage at The University Theatre, produced and directed fifteen student staffed, cast, and crewed feature films, writing most of the original screenplays. Just a few of his credits are available on IMDB.com.

He now lives in the Texas Panhandle where he writes his fiction. His webpage is http://www.jackrstanley.com.

ALSO BY THE AUTHOR:
NOVELS

ALSO BY THE AUTHOR

Novels

[Westerns]

Guns Along The Rio

West Of The Frio

A Hard Line Between The Rios

The Mormon Marshal

Along The Outlaw Trail

The Gavel and the Gun

13 Steps To Hell

Massacre At Going Snake

Incident at Lajitas

Pancho's Pilot

Return to Redemption

Occurrence At Latigo

The Dove And The Hardcase

The Widow And The Hardcase

Some Men Need Killin'

Ode To An Outlaw

Hanging In Temptation

Bad News In Temptation

Gunfighters in Temptation

First Train To Temptation

[Political Fiction]

The Reluctant President

The Reluctant Incumbent

The Reluctant Candidate

The Elected President

The Impeached President

[Vietnam]

Through A Lens Darkly: Vietnam

[Mysteries]

Murder In Muleshoe

Corpse In Canyon

The Lovecraft Murders

Short Stories

TALES FROM THE ALASKAN GOLD RUSH

Klondike Justice

Dangerous Camp On The Kenai

The Winds of Skagway

Screenplays

6 and 10

The 7th Luger

Afternoon Delight

Angel's Revenge

Between Love And Murder

Blood Drive

Death Scene

The Defection of Grigori Dorsky

The Evil Eye

Fatty and Hearst

Gideon: The Horse That Saved Texas

Hell In Paradise

Hollowpoint

Holiday For An Assassin

Horse Thief Hollow

Incident A tLajitas

Love, Lust, & Life

Mom & Apple Pye

Pancho's Pilot

The Prometheus Peril

The Rape of Sarah Quinn

Reservations

River of Tears

Seven Reasons Why

The Thing About Love

The Texas Rattlesnake Murders

Too Good To Be True

The Vampire Rose

A Violent End

The Virgin Casanova

Plays

Antigone In Texas

Cyrano

The Last Virgin From Las Vegas

The Seven Keys

The Unwed Widow

www.ingramcontent.com/pod-product-compliance
Lightning Source LLC
Chambersburg PA
CBHW032140170626
46808CB00006B/2313